MY FINE LADY

My Fine Lady

Yolanda Joe

DUTTON

DUTTON
Published by Penguin Group (USA) Inc.
375 Hudson Street, New York, New York 10014, U.S.A.
Penguin Books Ltd, Registered Offices: 80 Strand, London WC2R 0RL, England
Penguin Books Australia Ltd, 250 Camberwell Road,
Camberwell, Victoria 3124, Australia
Penguin Books Canada Ltd, 10 Alcorn Avenue, Toronto, Ontario, Canada M4V 3B2
Penguin Books (N.Z.) Ltd, Cnr Rosedale and Airborne Roads,
Albany, Auckland 1310, New Zealand

Published by Dutton, a member of Penguin Group (USA) Inc.

First Printing, March 2004
10 9 8 7 6 5 4 3 2 1

 REGISTERED TRADEMARK—MARCA REGISTRADA

LIBRARY OF CONGRESS CATALOGING-IN-PUBLICATION DATA

Joe, Yolanda.
   My fine lady / by Yolanda Joe.
      p. cm.
   ISBN 0-525-94808-2 (hardcover : alk. paper)
1. African American women singers—Fiction. 2. Teacher-student relationships—
Fiction. 3. African American families—Fiction. 4. Fathers and daughters—Fiction.
5. Voice teachers—Fiction. 6. Young women—Fiction. 7. Hip-hop—Fiction. I. Title.
PS3560.O242M9 2004
813'.54—dc22   2003017788

Printed in the United States of America
Set in Esprit Book

FOR MY NEPHEWS . . . DONALD AND DEVON . . .
WHO WILL ALWAYS HAVE MY LOVE AND MY PRAYERS

Thanks to my wonderful editor Laurie for her insight and her patience. You worked me for real this time, girl! I appreciate it.

Thanks to my agent and friend Victoria who works tirelessly to help make all of her writers successful. To her office crew Benee, Imani, and Roberta . . . y'all are dangerous.

Special thanks to the independent bookstore owners who struggle to keep their doors open and keep the work of black writers alive . . . and to the book clubs who are supportive and generous with their praise and their critiques.

And lastly, to all of the above, MUCH LOVE.

Prologue

Where does the hope for love begin?

In the heart? Where our insides are shaped like honeycombs with people buzzing in and out, turning our emotions into a syrupy sweet that drips out for us to taste?

Or is it in the mind? Where emotion sticks and stains like paint splatter against walls of doubt?

For nine-year-old Imani, it began both in her heart and in her mind. It was 1988, in a Maryland town that was the urban seam between Baltimore and D.C.

Imani was sitting on the front steps of her best friend's house with the other little girls in their downtown neighborhood. Imani had her ankles crossed and her knees up, needle-thin legs knitting the air. Her reddish-brown hair was unraveled and being tamed into long, even rows. Imani's best friend Shari was doing the braiding. A little boy named Taz stopped by to tease.

"How come your hair's always standing on top of your head? How come?"

"How come your stomach's always growling? I can hardly think in school 'cause your stomach's always growling."

All the girls laughed.

Taz was embarrassed. "Maybe you're just stupid."

Shari tugged on Imani's braids. "You gonna take that?"

Imani bolted off the steps and pushed Taz.

Taz wasn't about to be punked either. So he pushed her back.

Imani fell to the ground and bumped her elbow.

Shari dropped her comb, lunged off the steps, and slapped Taz upside his head.

Taz didn't want any part of Shari. She was two years older and, at age eleven, bigger and badder. But Taz knew someone bigger and badder than her. He threatened, "I'm telling Biggie."

"Biggie's your friend but he's my big brother, remember? How you gonna get Biggie on me? We family—*something you don't know nothing about.*"

Taz was really hurt now. Everybody knew he lived in the group home up the street. Why did Shari have to broadcast it? And he didn't mean to push Imani that hard. He didn't. Now she'd never like him. Never.

"Tell Imani you're sorry, Taz."

He shook his head no.

"Sorry didn't do it. He did," Imani yelled as she got up from the ground, tears streaming down her cheeks. "And he did it on purpose."

"Well, Taz," Shari reasoned, "you gotta give her something."

"Why, Shari?"

" 'Cause that's the way it goes. When a boy hurts a girl he's gotta give her something. That's what my mama says."

Imani dried her eyes. "Something like what?"

"Like flowers."

"I don't want no flowers."

Shari thought a second then whispered in Imani's ear. Imani blushed. "*I don't want none of that neither.*"

"Well my mama likes it."

"How do you know?"

"I heard her through the door hollering, *'Don't stop. Don't stop.'* "

The girls laughed.

Taz took off running. "I'll get you something good. I promise."

"But you don't know what I like!" Imani yelled after him.

"Imani, don't waste your time on that silly boy."

"I'm not. I don't like Taz."

As soon as Imani said that, a familiar voice came riding the wind. It was her father calling her from across the street. Imani saw the outline of his stout body. The down-and-out musician had his horn in one hand and was waving her home with the other hand.

"Aww shoot. I gotta go practice the piano."

"Skip it and come jump rope."

"Can't. See ya, Shari. Hey, don't forget we're sneaking out Saturday. Don't fake me out."

"I already told you, Imani, I'm in."

But at home Imani wanted out. She tried to talk her father Maceo into letting her skip piano practice.

"C'mon, Daddy, please? It's nice outside."

Her father Maceo was old school. He'd been born in the South and left home when he was sixteen to play with a band. The group traveled the single-lane highways of the delta, headlining joints in the backwoods where the crickets played the bass line. Maceo learned a lot about music and about life.

"I like any kind of music; you know that, Imani. But I promised your mama that I'd make sure you learned piano. That woman loved the sound of a piano."

Maceo knew he was slick. He knew that anytime he *really* wanted Imani to do something, all he had to do was say her mother did it or liked it. Imani never really knew her mother. A little girl like that would always want to latch on to something of her mom's . . . her likes . . . dislikes . . . maybe even her dreams.

Maceo missed his wife something fierce. She died when Imani was three from a sudden heart attack and lingering hard times.

They'd met fifteen years before, on Easter. The band had broken up. Maceo decided to take a part-time job playing for a little church in town. He had no intentions of staying. But you know love and its crazy ways. Love will make intentions grow roots.

The super soprano with the heavenly pipes was named Mae. Maceo just adored her gorgeous voice and her big pretty eyes. A shy but engaging personality sealed the deal. When Maceo looked at Imani now, he saw Mae's eyes and that same undeveloped talent. "What did I say about music, Imani? It's gotta be worked. So work."

Imani opened the songbook and her tiny shoulders slumped.

"Put in one hour. I'll be upstairs listening."

And drinking more than you're listening, Imani thought.

Imani began to play, hitting a foul note about every three or four keys. She'd much rather be listening to Salt 'n Pepa or Run DMC.

"Hey, Imani!"

Imani turned around and there was Taz at the window screen. He held up a lollipop.

Imani slid off the piano bench, happy for a reason to get away. She wanted the lollipop bad too—it was one of those big, swirled, multiflavored kinds. But the junior diva decided to give Taz a little attitude first. "Is that all you gonna give me?"

Taz heard Biggie say a true player always told a woman to take it or leave it *and she never left it.*

"Take it or leave it."

Imani took it.

"I don't hear nothing!" Maceo called out from upstairs. "Don't make me come down there."

Imani cocked her head to the side and twisted her lips. "See ya, Taz. I gotta go practice the stupid piano."

"I like piano."

"I don't. It's keeping me from playing."

"I could practice for you. Then we'd be cool about the pushing down thing."

Imani liked the idea. "For real?"

"Yeah."

"Okay. All you gotta do is play the first three songs in the songbook over and over again."

"That's it?"

"Oh and mess up a lot. I'll be back in an hour."

Imani lifted the screen and Taz crawled through the window.

Taz had taught himself to play by ear. It was a wonder, considering the kid boomeranged from one foster home to another with very little comfort or stability. He did live with a nice family once but unfortunately wasn't able to stay with them for very long. That family had an old piano in the basement. Taz was able to learn notes and tunes by listening to the radio. He took that knowledge and ran with it.

Taz began to make up songs. Raps. He loved rap music the best. The nice family hated to see Taz go to another foster home but they were moving out of state. Taz sulked when he found out, but didn't cry. After years of rejection, he was all cried out. The nice family gave him a Sony Walkman as a going-away present. He kept it under his pillow and listened to it at night. The music became a lullaby that chased away his loneliness.

Taz played the piano now, messing up for the first thirty minutes just like Imani said to do. Then he just forgot where he was and why. Taz began to play a song he heard on the radio. A Michael Jackson song. It had a booming beat he loved. Taz pounded the bass line on the piano and twinkled the keys.

He played and played . . . all the while he heard the pop star singing in his head . . . *Beat it* . . . *boom-dah-dee-dah boom-boomdaboom* . . . *boom-dah-dee-dah boom-boomdaboom* . . .

Outside, Imani was having a good old time playing with Shari and the girls. She was jumping double-dutch. Imani was in the middle of the rope, making up her own rhymes, jamming, her feet pounding the gravel pavement. Without warning, Imani's playmates dropped their rope ends and ran. Imani tumbled to the ground.

"Hey," she said jumping up with her hands on her hips like the little Sally Walker she was. "I turned for y'all. Come back here!"

Imani bent down to pick up the rope. She saw shoes. She'd know those shoes anywhere—a pair of dirty Nikes and a pair of black leather loafers with both heels on a flat.

Her throat went dry, but her eyes had to look.

Maceo had Taz by the back of the shirt so he couldn't run. Quiet as it's kept, she would've tried to run too if she had somewhere to go.

Maceo fussed at Imani all the way home, shaking her arm and fussing. He dragged Taz along; letting him know he was about one inch off his ass too.

Imani sat on the piano bench near tears.

"Don't start that crying or I'll give you something to cry about."

Imani sucked in air like she was drowning, her chest heaving, trying not to let a single tear fall.

Maceo took a drink out of the flask he kept in his back pocket. He drank and sized Taz up. "You're new around here. How old are you?"

"Nine. Me and Imani in the same grade."

"And y'all in the same trouble." Maceo took another long drink.

"I didn't do nothing."

"You ah story. It was all your idea, Taz."

"I didn't do nothing."

"Both of y'all, shut up. There's enough wrong to go around."

Taz's stomach growled.

"You hungry, son?"

"No."

"Daddy, they don't feed him half the time. He's a foster kid."

Taz hated her for saying that. For giving voice to the thing that he despised being most—a child that the world didn't value or love.

Maceo thought before taking another swig. "Tell you what, son . . ."

"Taz. My name is Taz."

"Okay, Taz. I'm gonna give you a job. I'll trade you dinner every night, starting tonight, if you come by here in the evening and give Imani piano lessons."

Taz acted like he was mulling the proposition over. He asked, "Can you cook?"

"Boy, I cook the best red beans and rice on the Maryland side of N'Orleans."

Maceo scooped Taz up—he almost cringed when he felt the boy's bony rib cage—and sat him down on the piano bench next to Imani. Taz put bass in his voice. "Okay, I'm the teacher. You play lousy, so from now on you need to practice two hours a day."

"Daddy!"

"Let Taz show you."

And from those lessons, the children's relationship would grow and grow, and so, too, would their dreams.

Children are blessed because they can dream with their eyes wide open.

That Saturday, Shari and Imani crept out of the house into the night just liked they'd planned. They rode their bikes to the secret spot far from home, their home where the streets are littered with garbage and the mailboxes are filled with government checks. Poor but proud, the neighborhood loved and cherished its children, children like Imani and Shari.

The two downtown girls went uptown, stopping outside the fence, which bordered a historically black university. Imani and Shari sat on the fence near a window.

Inside, the alumni charity ball was being held. The two little girls had ridden their bikes to see . . . to see the beautiful black women of various shades gowned in spectacular colors as they emerged from the limos and the Lincolns, latched on to the arms of tuxedoed black men.

Elegant. Glamorous. Magical. To the girls it seemed as if the pages of *Essence* magazine had come alive.

"Shari," Imani said to her best friend, "it's my turn to sit the closest."

They swapped places and Imani watched mesmerized, the moonlight dancing along the roots of her hair. Her heart leaped with excitement as she watched the women and men laugh and dance inside the ball. Imani gazed and whispered, "Someday . . . Someday . . ."

Children are blessed because they can dream with their eyes wide open.

Chapter One

Imani grew into a young woman who desired to be a star in the world and an endless torch in her lover's heart. Those conjoined dreams made up the center of her flower and its petals are all life's possibilities.

Imani's voice was velvet on fire. Her brown skin was minted copper by the sun. For her, the world was music. For her, the lover was Taz.

She glanced at him now from the stage of the underground music club. One look and Imani swallowed her nervousness and began to dance on magic legs.

Taz matched each of her fantasy moves step for step. Rugged hips rolled inside his baggy jeans. The hands that stroked her neck and back beneath the sheets now swung on beat at his sides. Taz's dark and brooding eyes focused with a hint of light. Why? Because he was turned on by the sight of Imani performing his music.

"If the world loved me, I'd bring it to its knees . . .
Making it my niggah, doin' as I pleased . . ."

Imani rapped his songs because Taz found unspeakable joy in beats and rhymes. She gave them voice, a voice that called out to their world.

Their world was right there, front and fabulous. Young men and women were jammed up against the stage. They let the grits meet the gravy, baby. They did their natural-born thing. Up against the wall. Up against other bodies. Up against the world hating on them with a passion. But it didn't matter. Because no matter what, they were still glorious.

It was a freeze-frame *I don't give a damn to the world*. It meant, *I'm getting my groove on whether you like it or not*. Because at that very moment, a generation's story was being sermonized onstage; the words were etched in culture, commandments of lifestyle documenting what it is to be inner-city hip and hopeless, fearless and fine.

Imani was *serious;* blowtorching out her rap the way ministers preach fire and brimstone from the Bible. The hip-hop congregation was digging on her sermon. But in his head Taz heard the gospel according to his critics. They had surfaced to the big time while Taz struggled.

Yo-yo-yo Taz. Your girl got skills no doubt. Makes your rhymes sound better than they are. But you gotta get harder, dog, if you wanna make it out of here. Your sound is too wangsta—wanna-be gangsta.

Nothing can bring down a person's mood faster than the thought of a bunch of folks hating on their dream. Pleased with Imani's performance, but not the fact that she went on first, or the chump change the club owner paid, the couple got in Taz's beat-up car and rode over to Lover's Leap to unwind. Imani tried to tighten up Taz's unhinged spirits.

"Baby, we're gonna make it. Stop worrying, hear? I don't care what nobody else says, we're gonna make it."

Taz smiled. Then he drew Imani to him. Taz pressed his tight muscular body up against hers. He kissed her passionately before stopping to whisper in her ear, "I wanna be with you. I wanna give you every inch of my talent; every inch of my body until you scream for more. I'm gonna show everybody I got juice by making you a star."

Imani was saved by Taz's words and washed in his rugged aroma. He smelled like natural earth in bloom. The pressure of his thighs against hers, the wetness of his lips against her skin made Imani wish for endless love the way children wish on a falling star.

Imani was a dreamer and she wore her hopes like speckled jewels. Anyone who met her was nearly blinded by the potential she showed and wound up hoping that the young diva conquered the world. Imani's desire for success was engaging.

Taz's desire for success was different. He had been orphaned by parents who were old enough to feel love, but who were too young to be responsible. So Taz felt life owed him.

It was in the world of rap that he wanted to thrive, to find intimacy. Beats and rhymes were his brothers and sisters. A song was the family he never had. He was determined to show that he belonged. His talent was awesome, the talk of the neighborhood and all the buzz in the underground music scene. But *somehow* Taz kept missing the big time. And that made his desire for success grow furiously.

Almost as furiously as the mad craving he had for Imani's body. She was a woman of stature; her breasts were mountains majesty and her hips curved from shore to shore. Her soft body was Taz's cushion. Her gentle spirit was his comfort. He wanted to shape, mold, and make Imani his own.

Taz peeled back the flimsy straps of Imani's tank top. The loosened material slipped down the way clouds slip away from the setting sun. Taz kissed every place that beckoned to him and left no pleasure call unanswered.

"Yo, Taz? Imani? That y'all?"

They both turned towards the voice that had come from the driver's side.

"It's me."

"Go away!" Taz yelled. He knew damn well who "me" was.
The car door was yanked open. The man with all the nerve
had a booming body that was big—*like powdah.* But all of his
facial features were Gerber Baby. This was Taz's best friend,
Biggie.

"Whatch'all doing?"

Imani quickly pulled up her top. Taz answered sarcastically.
"Whatdaya think we're doing? *She lost something and I'm helping
her find it.*"

"Need a hand looking, brah?" Biggie teased. "All I find all I
keep?"

Taz jumped up and smacked his head on top of the car door.
"Ouch!"

Biggie roared with laughter. He sang teasingly, "Hey, E-
mon-ie."

"Hey, Biggie," she growled. Imani slammed the door shut
after Taz fumbled his way out of the car.

"Aww, come on, baby, don't be like that!" Taz groaned at her.
He turned around and threw an elbow at Biggie's chest. "Niggah
what!"

Biggie laughed, falling on the car trunk. "What's up, player?"

"Nothing now. Get your fat butt off my ride."

"I ain't thinking about this wreckmobile. I'm about business
tonight. Here's the dealio. You've gotta do something about Maceo
and the money he owes."

Taz grabbed Biggie's arm and pulled him away from the car.
"C'mon, man, be cool. Imani doesn't know her father borrowed
that money or that he messed it up gambling either."

"That's a problem, dog. Maceo has gotta come up with some
cash or Mister Watson is gonna start tripping."

"Talk to him, Biggie."

"Like I haven't. That's all I've been doing is running my

mouth on Maceo's behalf. That's the only reason he's been able to get by this long."

"You've been holding it down for him?"

"Oh yeah, without a doubt. But time is ticking, Taz. The loan sharking business ain't no church charity. That Jeep I'm driving didn't come from the Goodwill. Mr. Watson wants to see some of his money or no telling what he'll make me do."

"You? But you're my best friend, Biggie. You wouldn't hurt Maceo; he's been like a father to me."

"Hurting Maceo ain't in my heart, but be real. You vouched for him and I vouched for you. Mr. Watson likes Maceo from way back, says he showed him how to hold a hand of cards and his liquor too. But a man's pity for another man don't roll down like water. It falls in drops."

"Like tears."

"Right. And I don't want us to be the ones crying for Maceo's ass."

"I feel you, Biggie."

"C'mon, Taz. Talk to him. You practically run the place for him. You make him pay the rent, bribe the liquor license man, pay all the insurance. He must have some money somewhere, don't he?"

"None."

"What about your girlie?"

"No! I just told you, Biggie; Imani ain't hip to none of this. And don't tell your big-mouth sister either. They're best friends and Shari can't hold water."

"Okay, relax. Let's split up. You go talk to Maceo. I'll go talk to Mr. Watson and stall for some more time. It's worth a shot."

Taz scratched his head then waved Biggie towards his Jeep. "Go ahead. I'll ride with you. You can drop me off first. I'll have Imani drive my car over to Shari's house and wait for me there."

"I know what you mean, Taz. A female can mess up a man's business in a heartbeat."

"Right. I don't want Imani nowhere around. You can drop me back over there later. I'll take her home then."

"I don't know, Taz. There's liable to be a whole lot of yacking behind this. What's Imani gonna say?"

Chapter Two

"Shari, I am sick of Taz and his shit."
Shari had on a nylon nightgown and was sitting at the dining room table painting her toenails with glitter polish. Her four-year-old daughter, nicknamed Baby, sat in a nearby booster chair. She liked to parrot people but *never ever* correctly repeated what they said.

"What's the matter now, Imani?"

"If Biggie says jump, Taz says into what Great Lake."

Shari stopped polishing and said in a sexy purr, "So, Biggie was a virus." Then she stood up and gyrated her hips. "And he wiped out Taz's hard drive."

"Forget you, Shari. And stop showing off. Everybody knows you're studying computers in night school."

"And foreign languages too."

"How do you say you're pissed off in a foreign language?"

"Oy vay!"

Baby sang out, "Oil of Olay!"

The two women laughed.

"Imani, you might as well stop buggin' about it. You know Taz. He's been running behind my brother for the longest. Biggie was always protecting him from the bad boys on the block when we were kids."

Imani sucked her teeth and plopped down in a chair.

"The same way I protected you from those face-scratching bathroom girls in high school."

"You were one of those face-scratching girls in the bathroom."

Shari faked surprise in her very best inner-city French accent. *"Sacre bleu!"*

Baby sang, "Socks blue!"

Shari leaned over, kissed her little girl, and nodded towards Imani. "Look at Auntie Imani. Ain't she tripping? I *was* a bathroom girl *back then*—but this is now."

"What's the difference?"

"Today, I'm a lady."

Shari made a demonstrative turn while throwing a Halle Berry glance over her shoulder. She begged pardon, "Oops-ie-'scuse!" Shari had stuck cotton between her toes to let the polish dry. She popped up on the back of her heels and waddled towards the kitchen like a duck with a stick up its butt.

"That's how a lady walks?"

"If she has polish on her toes and says Oops-ie-'scuse, yes."

Baby sang, "Whoochie coo!"

Shari grabbed beers for herself and Imani.

"I'm telling you, Shari, it ain't right. Taz and Biggie are up to *something* in that studio at night. Taz says those are Biggie's hos running in and out of there."

"Knowing my brother? Probably."

"Birds of a feather *hunt pussy together.* What am I gonna do about Taz?"

"Imani, girl, you've got to put it on him."

"What?"

"It!" Then Shari got up, dropped one hand on her hip like a handle, and swiveled and dipped around 180 degrees to a stop. *"It!* C'mon, girl."

Imani got up and began the swivel hip rock, "Put *it* on him . . ."

"And . . . ," Shari interjected with a wink, "afterwards say . . ."

"Oops-ie-'scuse!" they sang out together, and fell back down into their chairs.

And it was in that same chair that Imani dozed off to sleep while watching a movie. When she awoke, it was almost one o'clock in the morning. Shari and Baby both had gone to bed. Where is Taz? Imani wondered. She decided then and there to drive herself home. Taz would just have to get his car later.

Imani was shocked as she drove up to her building. It wasn't the shattered glass on the street or the stained paper bags in the gutter.

Imani was used to that.

And it wasn't the hustlers standing on the corner when she got out of the car or the sounds of domestic violence pumping out of the pores of the apartment bricks. It was the growing flames that were beginning to paint hot orange streaks across the sky.

Club Maceo was on fire.

What fate brings humanity has to accept. But when the human heart fights back with courage, sometimes fate's misfortune flames out.

And so Imani glared defiantly at the blaze that had begun to engulf Club Maceo and willed herself not to panic.

The glaring orange-tongued fire licked the rear of the building hoping to taunt Imani into a spiraling frenzy of fear. Instead of fear, poignant questions began to throb inside her brain. *Where's Daddy?* she thought. *He's always smoking and drinking in bed.*

"Is somebody in there?" a bystander asked. "I think somebody's in there, y'all!"

The possibility wavered in Imani's mind like the flames that looped along the prism edges of the shattered windows. She uttered the word "Daddy!" before running towards the burning building. Imani ran with a purpose as pure as the crescent moon above and as steady as a heroic heartbeat.

Imani only stopped short when she saw Biggie come running out of the alley nervously checking behind him all the while. He tossed away a rag he had in his hand.

"Biggie!"

Startled, the big man froze in his tracks. "Imani!"

"Where's my daddy?"

"I don't know."

"Oh God, he's inside!" Imani jerked around and made a dash for the door, a door with smoke billowing out of it.

Biggie tried to stop her but she slipped through his grasp. Fate's black magic pulled the curtain and Imani disappeared through the smoky doorway. Everyone who saw gasped in fear— everyone.

Inside, the life-snatching flames of the fire swirled all around Imani. She tried to look through the pumping smoke that was clouding the room. Visibility was still possible and her heart pounded as she called out her father's name.

Suddenly Imani was turned around. Where was the door? To the right? To the left? She didn't know where to move and began to feel lightheaded. Imani began to slowly fall to the floor.

Falling . . . falling.

Her head felt lighter and lighter; none of her thoughts had weight . . . none of her limbs had strength.

Falling . . . falling.

As Imani sank the last few inches onto the field of black smoke beneath her, two hands reached down and caught her like a ballplayer making a shoestring catch.

Imani watched the room wobble up and down as she was rushed to safety in the arms of a fireman. Once outside, she gobbled at the fresh air, and it felt like cream rolling down her throat. The fireman eased Imani to a sitting position inside the open door of the ambulance. "You okay?" he asked.

"Yeah. Gotta catch my wind."

The fireman grunted and rushed off. The next face she saw belonged to Taz. He looked into her frightened eyes and read her thoughts like they were printed on a page. "Maceo's across the street at the pool hall. He's fine."

"Good thing too." Biggie coughed. "This fire ain't no joke."

Imani lifted her head the way a bird lifts its beak towards an approaching storm. "Taz. My notebook. It's still in there."

"Relax, baby. Forget about it for now."

"But it's got all my rhymes!"

"Hold on." Taz held Imani. "It'll be okay. Just wait and see."

And the waiting of time often drips traumatic and caustic to the soul. There are so many fears because of what is being lost. The items of our lives that would bring a laugh from a worldly appraiser actually bring tears to our own eyes; that's because, to us, they are priceless. So Imani openly shed tears for her mother's treasure chest that was lost.

The chest was filled with her baby keepsakes; filled with the only remaining copies of a seldom-sold album her mother recorded back in the late seventies, and with church programs from her grandmother's Sunday concerts when she sang for the collection plate and not the pocketbook; filled with publicity photos of her father's failed solo career.

Imani held one of those photos now, in the wake of the fire, as she stood on the singed floor of the back room of Club Maceo. Firefighters were rummaging around looking for spots that could flare up.

Imani clutched the frame, in it a photo she imagined her mother in heaven must have taken off the wall and held, keeping it safe from the fire just for her. It was Imani's favorite photo of her dad. He was about thirty years old, in a tux, holding his horn, his hair bootblack, and his teeth pearly and square. The early morning sun cast a beam directly on the photo; the glass frame sparkled. Imani could see her reflection and just over her shoulder now, her father's image today. *What a contrast.* Age had heavily seasoned his hair with salt. He was missing three front teeth, and smelled of rum with a failure chaser.

"Honey," Maceo said, "you're all cried out. And trembling."

"Mama's albums are gone . . ."

"I know." He hugged Imani. "But we'll always hear her in our hearts."

"And the club. How you gonna make a living, Daddy?"

"The whole building didn't go. Most of it's still good."

Taz was milling around the rubble too. "Good thing I made you pay the insurance, Maceo."

"I appreciate that now. That insurance money is gonna save the day sho' as I'm standing here."

A firefighter offered his two cents. "You might be slow getting it, mister."

"Why?"

"Never mind."

"This is my place, burned up as it is, but it's mine. I've a right to know. Speak your mind, son."

"Well, fact is . . . This fire looks suspicious. We got the call early enough. But somehow the fire spread quickly anyway. The back half of the building took a hit. And you know what? We found some rags out back. They were soaked with alcohol."

An image flashed in Imani's head. *She saw Biggie running towards her before tossing away a rag.*

"This is a bar," Taz reasoned to the firefighter. "There's supposed to be liquor in here. Those rags were probably tossed by the cleanup guy. Too lazy to slam dunk 'em in the garbage can. Ain't nobody set no fire in here. You straight tripping, man."

"Okay, okay. Don't shoot the messenger. But I'm telling you, they're still gonna want to take a good long look at this one."

Imani grabbed Taz and pulled him aside. "I saw Biggie running out of the alley. From the back where the fire started."

"So what? He was looking for me. To take me over to Shari's to get you."

"But Taz, when Biggie saw me, he got this funny look on his face."

"Because you were supposed to be at Shari's. That's all. He was surprised to see you."

"Naw, Taz, I saw him with a rag in his hand. He threw it away—"

"Hold up. What you tryin' to say, Imani?"

"I think Biggie set the fire."

"*What?* Why would he?"

For the life of her Imani couldn't think of a single reason why.

"You're stressed out, Imani. Biggie is my boy. He's your best friend's brother. Stop tripping."

"I guess you're right, Taz." Imani walked back over to her father. "Daddy, we'll just have to do what we can to make ends meet until the insurance money comes in. All of us. I'm gonna do everything I can . . . street rapping plus work some more hours at Shari's salon. I'm up for the challenge."

It was clear to Imani that she faced a challenge. But how could she know that in a couple of weeks she would be in a battle that, if won, would change her life forever?

Chapter Three

Imani's battle would be fought on a field of promise, just like the one fought on decades before when a mecca of higher education was being born. Less than five miles away from Imani's 'hood was a tree-lined campus built with the cracked palms and whip-scarred backs of emancipated slaves. The dream for it all came from colored activists like Fredrick Douglass. The money came from white abolitionists. They called the university Arlington.

Now, more than 125 years later, the historically black college's enrollment was down. The endowment was shriveling. The music department and its stellar reputation was the heartbeat that kept the university alive. And within that department was a rising academic star, Orenthal Ellis Hopson.

He looked more like a young movie star than a scholar. Hopson had cream-in-the-coffee eyes with long lashes and a disarming gaze. His smile was like a cluster of stars. He had skin that made ladies on the street want to stroke his face to prove that it was as smooth as it looked. By the grace of heredity, Hopson had been blessed with strong locks of hair that gallantly formed a perfect warrior Afro.

To be blunt, Mother Nature had just been darn right good to

the brother. Better than he could ever be to himself. Hopson wanted to appear stately, more mature than he was because he was a prodigy and had achieved academic stardom far earlier than most.

So the young brother played his true spirit and constructed a knockoff image for himself. He hid his dazzling eyes behind plain glasses, wore loose old-man suits on his buff body, and kept a bubbly personality in check.

Hopson let his gaze fall and land now on each of the students in the advanced jazz band. They played for him, these sons and daughters of a stolen people. For their ancestors, a sameness of skin bound them, and a difference in tribal tongues separated them. But in the sailing belly of slavery's whale, and on the shores of bondage, drums and song became their universal language.

The centuries since had changed the rhythms and rhymes. What once had been the lifeline of an entire race, for the most part, had now become money melodies for mainstream America.

So these talented sons and daughters played Arlington's school song from a foreign, emotionless place. They just didn't care, so their notes lacked passion. This combination of *dissin' and disdain* caused Professor Hopson to explode.

"Stop! Wait! Everybody's off but Dee."

Dee played in the horn section, a plain black girl from the Midwest. She had a soft voice and had grown up in a sheltered environment. Her clothes were not hip and she was painfully shy. Her struggle was to fit in. Professor Hopson loved to praise Dee. And getting a lot of praise wasn't helping her cause with the band's cool crew.

"What about some spirit? Where's the heart of this song, people?"

"In the med lab," a handsome young man in the horn section joked. "Still in the frog!"

The class roared with laughter.

"Very funny, Ahmad. Where is the love, people? The men and women who built this university sang this song when the doors opened. There were no cell phones to tell anybody about it. No e-mails. Just exuberant voices rising up with joy because they had accomplished something no other generation had."

"Professor Hopson," Ahmad defended himself, "we know the song is part of the school's history. But why does history have to be so dry?"

"Yeah," Dee managed to say. She had a mad crush on Ahmad and would say anything to please him. "The song is dry, Professor."

"It's not dry. It's a classic. Ahmad, you're band president. You need to set a better example."

"I am, Professor. I'm being real. Hip-hop is what's happening."

Hopson placed his wooden director's wand on the podium in front of him. "I can't believe you're disrespecting the school like this, Ahmad."

"But all we want to do is rock the pep rally showcase next week. We can do a real hip version of the school song."

"No way."

"Why, Professor?"

"Because there's tradition to uphold. Leave the head bobbing and booty shaking to the drum line. We're the jazz band."

"Meaning?"

"Meaning we're better than that. We're more talented. More—"

"Boring."

"Drop it, Ahmad."

"But I'm being real, Professor; everybody's gonna be hating on us! The students are tired of the school song."

"Not if it's done right. Let me show you."

Hopson swung his suit jacket away from his shoulders the way Superman flips back his cape. He grabbed his horn the way the Count of Monte Cristo grabs a sword. He grinned like Louie Armstrong, then played like Miles Davis.

And what came from that horn was a spirit that sprinkled a lyrical blessing all around the room. Hopson had begun playing the piano at age three. He brought tears to the eyes of the women at Bible study. By age twelve he was playing symphonies. The next year he discovered the horn and immediately fell in love with the sleek, pewter steel that returned his passionate kisses with the sound of sensual melodies.

Hopson finished playing. Dee moaned, "That was beautiful."

And because of the way she said it, and her expression afterwards, so mousy and so geeky . . . *everyone laughed.*

Ahmad laughed the loudest before agreeing with Dee. "Professor, she's right. You've got skills. Mad skills. But let me stand up at the pep rally and play that and see if I don't get booed and laughed at all over the yard."

A drummer hit the cymbals. Then gave Ahmad a fist-tapping five.

Hopson fought the mutiny. "Well Ahmad, I'm sure your enormous ego can take it."

The class started to hiss and tease, "Faced by the professor! *Ooooohhh!*"

"Come on. Settle down. Let's try it again, from the top. Some emotion this time, please."

Professor Hopson began to direct.

Then from the doorway came the sound of a horn playing a swinging version of the Arlington song. The notes were the same but the feeling was not. It was a bit reckless, windless, fly, current but not substantive, yet somehow, extremely engaging.

The students began to piggyback off this hip version.

Professor Hopson snapped his wooden director's wand against the side of the desk. The students dropped their tempo and resumed the tradition.

The competitive horn blared louder, hipper.

The students picked up that tempo again.

Professor Hopson glared at the doorway. Another professor was now walking into view. He leaned on the doorway, playing his horn, knowing he was stealing the show. This was Professor Rick Sherman—Hopson's colleague and fierce rival.

It would be a *lowdown showdown*. Because whenever the two men were in the same room together, there was always some one-upmanship going on.

Professor Sherman had been a bit envious of Professor Hopson long before he ever got to Arlington. That's because Chairman Perkins gave the prodigy professor the very best music majors to mentor. He also got other campus perks right off the bat without paying his dues. Plus Sherman learned that Hopson's people had money and plenty of it. *Spoiled*, Sherman thought. But once they met, he realized that there was something about Professor Hopson that he liked. Each man respected the other's skills in music, but each thought himself just a little bit better. So it was always a competition between the two whenever the chance arose.

Hopson stalked over to the doorway and yanked Professor Sherman's horn down. Sherman, around thirty-five, a plain yet expressive face, hip in dress, confident in attitude, bucked his eyes and let a sly grin spread across his face.

The students stopped playing.

"Problem, Hopson?"

"Yes. What are you doing in my classroom?"

Sherman sucked his teeth. Then he looked around at the students and winked. "I thought I heard a funeral march, so I came to pay my last respects."

The students began to jeer. *"Oooooooh!"*

Hopson pushed Sherman out of the classroom. Sherman allowed it, smiling a goofy grin, while backpedaling like a drunk out into the hallway.

"Oooooooh!"

Hopson slammed the door behind them. "What's wrong with you? You're worse than a kid, always playing around."

"C'mon, Hopson. You never let the students have any fun. And it wouldn't hurt you to have some fun too. You're all uptight because you're the Ellington Fellow."

"That's not true."

"Oh no?" Sherman stepped back and gave Hopson the once-over. "You're the youngest person to get the fellowship. You're barely twenty-five. And you walk around here in those old-man suits, trying to act like old Chairman Perkins."

"That's a lie."

"Oh yeah? I'm thirty-five and I know more about the current music trends than you do."

"All right. I'll give you that."

"And who had more students on the dean's list? And more music majors to graduate *on time?*"

"You did, Sherman. But who had more articles published last year?"

Professor Sherman had to concede that point. Professor Hopson grinned.

"Don't gloat so much, man. That's only because I didn't have the time. I extended my office hours last year. I had to make sure all the seniors were able to get out of here."

"You should have been more worried about getting published. Sometimes, Sherman, it seems like you don't want to get tenure."

"I've had to work like a dog to come up through the ranks here at Arlington. I'm top dog in the music department. Don't worry about me. You're an up-and-comer, true. But I'm not about to let you show me up."

"You're not?" Professor Hopson said with a cocky smile.

"No, I'm not," Professor Sherman sassed. "I didn't grow up with a silver spoon in my mouth like you. I'm from the streets and I play to win." Professor Sherman tipped his horn. "But I like your grit."

Hopson nodded appreciatively, then headed back into the classroom.

The students ran back to their seats after they had eaves-dropped through the door.

Professor Hopson raised his director's wand again. "From the top."

Professor Sherman was standing in the doorway, horn down, playing possum.

The students cut sly glances at one another. Then they began playing Professor Sherman's version of the Arlington song.

"Stop it. Stop—it!" Professor Hopson yelled. "Listen, you will play the song the way I say *or* you'll fail my class. Is that clear?"

The students suddenly became wide-eyed and silent.

"Now what? Are you deaf?"

Chairman Perkins answered for the students. "Certainly not."

Hopson could only manage a blank stare as he turned around to look at the department chairman now standing behind him.

Chairman Perkins had a white soul patch, white temples, and a perfectly round Afro. His weathered face held piercing eyes. A pronged cane aided his walk. His vested suit, although well kept, was tweed and strictly fifties-style. He had the stance and the class of a Sidney Poitier.

"Professor Hopson, we need to talk."

"But what about my class?"

"Professor Sherman will take over. In fact, it seems like he already has."

Hopson followed Chairman Perkins out. He stopped for a second, just long enough to whisper to Sherman, "Next time."

Sherman whispered back, "Bring it."

Chapter Four

After Sherman told Hopson to bring it, Chairman Perkins told him to get with it.

Everyone on Arlington's campus recognized the stately department chairman as he walked across the yard with his hopeful protégé. Or at least the man Chairman Perkins had hoped would be his successor when he picked Orenthal Hopson for the prestigious Ellington Teaching Fellowship last year.

"You're the youngest person we've ever chosen. I'm beginning to think I pushed the committee into making a mistake."

Professor Hopson cut his eyes at the old guy. *Always demanding,* he thought. *And always riding me.* "Chairman, I know you don't believe in my research."

"How can I? Your theory is outrageous, Hopson! What is it again? Wait a second, I know: Music can alter an individual's personality, their entire behavior despite at what point they're introduced to it."

"Right. What's so crazy about that?"

"A baby introduced to music will have a better-developed brain. Makes sense to me. A child who masters an instrument will have a stronger sense of confidence. I buy that too."

Hopson picked up the argument. "But someone who has already fully developed as an individual . . ."

". . . past puberty cannot be profoundly changed by music. Period."

"But they can, Chairman Perkins! Think: Haven't you ever been moved to tears by a song?"

"Yes."

"Haven't you ever been depressed and music has lifted you up?"

"Sure."

"Then if music can alter that state on a temporary basis, if duly applied why couldn't it work on a grander scale, and change someone's personality—their outlook on life completely?"

"It's too easy, Hopson. Can't you see that? If it were that easy, then all we'd have to do is pipe music into the prisons. Then all the criminals would be reformed."

"That's silly."

Chairman Perkins stopped and glared at Professor Hopson.

"Sorry, Chairman."

"Not as sorry as I am, Professor." They began to walk again. "I was hoping that you could come up with something more solid for the grant competition. You do realize—"

"I know, Chairman. I know. The Federal Music Grant is the most prestigious in the country."

"Not to mention worth two hundred thousand dollars to the university that wins it. Arlington needs that money. So it'll be either your paper we submit or Professor Sherman's."

The words erupted inside Hopson's brain. He *did not* want that. That would be the biggest topper of them all. And Sherman would never let him forget it—no matter what.

"Are you deaf?" Chairman Perkins asked, mimicking the professor's earlier taunt to his students.

"No, I'm not. And you're not being fair. My theory is right."

"I'm not convinced. Can we take a chance on it? We've got to do our best to win. The school needs the money, Professor."

"It'll win. I just know it."

But Chairman Perkins was no longer listening. He was drawn into a growing battle. And soon Hopson was too; drawn into a battle of wills, a battle that would dramatically change his life.

Chairman Perkins and Professor Hopson would witness that battle, watching now as it boiled over right in front of them. Next to the student dorm, a security guard was blocking the path of a young woman. Neither man had ever seen her before.

She was dressed ultrahip. She had on a Chicago White Sox game jersey with a white T-shirt underneath. Her baggy, boy jeans were tie-dyed black and white, and she wore some spike-heeled boots. Her thick hair was braided simply from the front of the scalp all the way to the back. A black bandana circled her forehead. Two golden hoop bangles circled from her earlobes to the top of her shoulders. It was Imani, and the school's black Barney Fife was berating her.

"Listen, you townies don't belong on campus. You roam around here, trying to steal stuff . . ."

"Steal!" Imani threw her head back and the word snapped out of her mouth like spit. "Ain't nothing around here I want."

"Then get off the property."

"Like you're a student. What do they pay you, huh? Minimum wage? You're a townie just like me. What's up with that?"

The security guard grabbed Imani's arm and jerked her around.

"Hey," Chairman Perkins shouted, "stop that!" His pronged cane kicked up dust as he walked as briskly as he could towards the brawl.

Professor Hopson hung his head on the spot and thought, *Now what?* He dallied before inching over to where the trouble was.

"Let that young woman go!"

"But Chairman Perkins, you don't understand . . ."

Imani jerked away and ran around the corner.

"See? Now she's gone. I'm supposed to keep them from cutting across campus and stuff. I've got orders."

"But you don't have manners. Here at Arlington, every man is a gentleman. So whether you are a student or a professor or a security guard like yourself, we treat all women like ladies. Is that understood?"

"Yes, sir."

Professor Hopson was eager to get back to his theory. "Chairman, can we go somewhere and talk? Over coffee maybe?"

"What's that noise?" Now a growing sound caught Chairman Perkins's attention.

In the distance, a herd of students had gathered in a brick enclave behind the dining hall. It was the sound of unchained rhythm—beats tapped out on the underside of thighs like the old hambone days of the South, sticks against empty plastic buckets, the new drums of ghetto playlots, and exuberant cries of "unhuh, un-huh yeah. Un-huh, un-huh yeah."

"What's going on over there, Professor?"

"Nothing. Just a student thing. Now as I was saying . . ."

"What kind of a student thing?"

Hopson's shoulders slumped. He answered exasperated, "They collect money and whoever raps the best wins the pot."

"Interesting."

"Not really."

Chairman Perkins walked over anyway. Professor Hopson followed reluctantly. They found a spot in the rear of the crowd to stand and observe.

Imani stepped up on the wooden picnic bench. She worked her arms to loosen up a bit and the game jersey floated defiantly on her shoulders. She dug in with her spike-heeled boots like a batter in the World Series.

As Imani stood up on the table some of the excitement escaped out of the crowd. A group of coed divas sat on the front table in their very best hanging jury form. They were a costly crew. They had Coach bags and Gucci loafers. One of the *pretty on the outside but evil on the inside* girls yelled, "Townie!" The mob gaped at Imani.

Their disdain only fueled the urban diva. She looked at each and every one of them, her gaze like a scepter knighting their shoulders. Her confidence burst through her person—through her dazzling smile, her eyes, through her defiant stance.

The adversarial silence of the students, in an instant, was transformed into an edgy murmur anticipating the performance to come. Imani began to rock back and forth to a rhythm in her head. Directed by her eyes, the students began to move with Imani, becoming her choir. Next they began to clap.

"Yes-yes-y'all," she thanked them. "Yes-yes."

Imani began to rap, in a throaty voice, two octaves below her normal register. The words burned with honesty, talked about the poverty her eyes had seen, the sorrow her lips had cried, and the courage her heart had felt. In the middle she crooned two notes, going up then down the scale. Next, mixed in with more rap, were the rough vowels of the street, profanity here and there as punctuation, but still, all in all, riveting.

Imani was so good that everyone who performed before her appeared to be ill, and the one person who performed after her seemed to be ailing.

At the end of it all, the crowd cheered and wolfed for Imani, electing her the champion and filling her jean pockets with greenbacks. Imani glowed, "Right, right y'all."

Chairman Perkins turned to Professor Hopson. "Do you really stand by your theory?"

"Yes."

"You want me to enter it in the grant contest instead of Professor Sherman's?"

"Yes."

"You're sure it'll win?"

"Without a doubt."

"Then prove it, Professor."

"How?"

"With her." Chairman Perkins pointed at Imani. "That rapper. Introduce her to the classics. Train her with the music of Basie and Ellington, then turn her into an elegant jazz singer. Do that, and it'll prove your theory is correct. Then I'll enter your paper."

"But Chairman, I can't."

"Why not?"

Suddenly the image of Professor Sherman flashed through Hopson's head. His gut churned. He refocused on Chairman Perkins. "It's a deal."

"Good."

"But on two conditions, Chairman. One: She can't know about the bet. And two: You can't be the sole judge of whether or not she's changed."

"Are you trying to say I'd cheat?"

"I'm trying to say that one man's princess is another man's frog."

Chairman Perkins laughed hardily. "Okay. Then we'll have her perform at the President's Charity Ball—that's three months away."

"Three months!"

"What's the matter, Hopson? Like the students say, can't you back your stuff up?"

Hopson glared at the chairman before squaring his shoulders. "I'll back it up. If there's one thing I hate, it's losing."

Then the two men shook hands and turned towards Imani, whose beauty rose like a light above the throng of students surrounding her.

"A penny for your thoughts, Professor."

"I know I can change her life if I get the chance. But the question is, how can I reach her?"

Chapter Five

The reach of our hands is limited like the heavy-laden branches of summer trees. But the reach of our minds is limitless, with no true beginning or end like the galaxy that stretches far above our heads. The stars there burn with promise and, despite distance, give us a nightly glimpse of what miracles are. This is a gift from God, allowing us to regularly visualize what is possible.

"You have star quality," Professor Hopson said to Imani as the students made their way to class and she got her money together.

She hardly heard him, not looking up but counting, "Ten, fifteen, twenty . . . Huh, better than passing the hat outside the bus station all day."

"Miss," Professor Hopson said, touching her arm.

"Back up off me! I'm tired of you campus security guards. Why y'all always gotta be bothering us?"

"Whoa, whoa." Hopson turned her towards him and their eyes met. "Do I look like security to you?"

"No, you ain't security."

She examined his soft eyes and his creamy skin. Imani checked his shoulders out as they managed to show a fine line underneath that old played-out suit jacket. The man had some height to him. Imani liked that. But he looked way too corny— just like TV's Negro nerd, Erkel. But even Erkel's alter ego was fine once he got out of those punk-ass clothes and welfare eyeglasses. Although Imani acknowledged Professor Hopson's good looks, she knew he was uptown and she was downtown. He was university and she was townie. To Imani, that meant be on guard. "So you're not trying to run me off?"

"No, I'm actually trying to get you to stay so we can talk. I'm Professor Orenthal Hopson."

Imani laughed.

"What's so funny?"

"That name. You must have gotten your ass kicked in school."

Hopson kept his anger in check.

"What's your name?"

"Imani."

Hopson started to laugh.

"What's so funny?"

"That name. Sounds like an extra in an Indiana Jones movie."

Imani rolled her eyes, grabbed her bag, and started walking. Hopson quickstepped behind her.

"Wait, Imani—we got off to a bad start."

"You ain't lying."

"I'm a music professor here. Have you ever heard of Count Basie?"

Imani played him off.

"*Hello?*"

"Yeah, I heard of him. My old man listens to him all the time."

"Well your boyfriend has taste."

"My *old man* is my father, Maceo."

"Sorry."

"Have you heard of Wynton Marsalis?"

"Yeah, my man don't like him too much."

"Well, your father's probably a traditionalist."

"*My man* is my boyfriend, Taz." She stopped and rolled her eyes. "Do you have ah clue?" Then she walked off before he could answer.

Hopson grabbed Imani by the arm. "If you'd stand still like a lady and use proper English, we could hold a conversation."

"Kiss my ass."

"How does your mother like that mouth?"

Imani caught her next nasty retort. She paused, her words slow. "My mother . . . is dead."

"Oh . . . I'm sorry. I didn't know."

"Forget about it. Listen, I ain't trying to get into no drama. I've got a ton of stuff to do and I'm late for work. So listen here, I didn't mean to jump on you like that. Sorry."

"Apology accepted."

"Then we're all good?"

"Absolutely."

"Cool. I'm out."

"Wait." Hopson cut in front of her. "I think you can be a star. Let me help you."

"You own a record label?"

"No."

"You know Master P?"

Hopson shrugged. "He's doing telephone commercials."

"That's *Mister T.*"

"Oh."

Imani giggled. "Listen, my boyfriend Taz produces all my stuff. He is the shit. We're gonna have our own record label one day. The biggest and baddest rap label in the world."

"Rap is a waste for you, Imani."

"What? *Pah-lease.* Rap is cutting edge. It's real. It's the voice of the streets."

"But your voice sounds like it's from heaven."

"Can't be. 'Cause right now my life ain't blessed. My raps talk about the real deal in the world. The stories that play out three miles away from this college campus with its plantation-style buildings and its siddity rich kids."

"Imani, this is a historically black college. There are no deep pockets here, just brains and talent. Most of our students are on some kind of scholarship. And what does place have to do with music anyway?"

Imani paused, faced him squarely, then leaned back on her right hip. "Music *is* place, man. It's about what's around you. 'Cause what's around you gets in you. That's why music touches people."

"Wrong. Talent touches people. The way you stole the show today had nothing to do with place. You could have been in the middle of a cornfield in Iowa or by the pyramids in Egypt. *Anywhere.* You've got talent, Imani."

She blushed, but still quickly moved on. Hopson followed her like a bloodhound.

"Listen to me, Imani. I want to showcase that talent in its richest light. I want to give you a new look and a jazz act that'll be the talk of the town."

"Jazz? That's my daddy's thing; like thirty-three LPs and deuce-and-a-quarter cars. I'm a *rapper.*"

"You're a *singer.* I heard your voice. Let me help you."

"Listen . . . ah . . . professor . . . uh . . . what's-your-name . . ."

"Orenthal Hopson."

Imani smiled again at his funny-sounding name and shortened it. "Listen, Hops, I need to make money. Playing dress-up and pretend is for little girls who have time to dream."

"You're wrong, Imani. This dream can be real. Take my card. Let's set up a time when we can meet and iron things out. I want you to work for me as my assistant, and at the same time we can work on your music."

"Oh, hold up. You talking about some cheddar?"

"I'd have to check on the money part, Imani. But I'm sure we can figure out a way to get you a little something—"

"I get it," Imani waved off the card. *The townie will take the big-time professor's crumbs, huh?"*

"I didn't say that. I don't play people cheap."

"Is that right?"

"That's right, so your answer is yes."

"Wrong. My answer is no."

"Why?"

" 'Cause . . ."

" 'Cause what, Imani?"

" 'Cause I don't wanna. What's the matter, Hops? Nobody's ever told you no before?"

"Not when God knows the answer should be yes."

Out of the corner of her eye, Imani saw the bus coming. She made a dash for it. "That's my ride!"

"Wait!"

Hopson took off after her. Imani made the bus just as the doors were closing.

"Wait! How can I get in touch with you?"

Imani waved good-bye. The bus pulled away and Hopson was unable to take his eyes off her.

"Aww," a female student yelled running up. "Missed my bus. Was that Imani, Professor?"

"You know her?"

"Yeah. She works at the salon where I go to get my hair done."

"Thank God. Tell me: How can I find her?"

Chapter Six

"We gonna all find ourselves in the po' house." Shari's voice crackled with frustration. "Am I the only person in this beauty shop who's 'bout business? Imani, you're late."

"Shari . . . now, you know . . . I'm never late."

"You are today."

" 'Cause I was out hustling my music." Imani opened the door to one of the lockers that Shari had installed in the back room of the beauty shop. "I finally had a good day too. I hit Arlington U. Had some trouble with a guard, but I ended up making some paper."

"I'm trying to get paid too." Shari rolled her eyes. "Let's go." She threw Imani a smock.

Imani caught it. Shari scooted back out front. *What's her trip?* Imani thought. When she looked up at the sign-in board she knew. *Damn.* The other two shampoo girls were out sick, *again.*

Imani hustled back out front. The first person to greet her was Shari's mother, Ma June.

"They waiting on you, girl," Ma June said. She sat in the front booth, answering phones and checking in customers. "They waiting on you like a pack of wolves."

Five women were sitting in the front chairs of the beauty shop. Every last one of 'em had a head of hair that was a hot mess, and not one of 'em had a pretty look on her face. Imani tried to play it off.

"All right, who's next?"

"Me!" Two women stood up at the same time.

"I'm Minnie's two o'clock."

"I'm her one o'clock. Like it matters. She's not even back from lunch yet." The woman's phone went off. She looked. "Speak of the devil and she sends a text message." She read out loud. " 'On my way: Baby's daddy acting up. Minnie.' "

"Ain't that nerve?" Minnie's two o'clock growled. "Paging us at *her job* talking about she's on *her way.*"

Ma June tossed in her two cents: "Y'all know Minnie is trifling."

Ma June had a feathered haircut with a flaming-red dye job. Her work wardrobe consisted of all the hip stuff the boosters brought into the shop to sell—whether it looked too young for her or not. "Minnie is trifling as can be." Ma June shook the bangles on her wrists for emphasis. "But the child can do some hair."

One o'clock agreed. "You right, Ma June. *Welp, let's get this shampoo on the road.* I've been here the longest, so I'm next."

"Wrong," Two o'clock growled. "I'm a weekly customer with a standing appointment, so I'm next."

They grumped at each other for a minute, then looked at Imani.

"Nah-nah. I don't wanna get in the middle of no drama."

"Don't start none, won't be none." One o'clock had her hands on her hips. "You decide and we'll go along with that."

"Y'all sure?"

"Sure," they both said.

The phone rang. Ma June answered it. "Imani, telephone. Professor somebody."

Imani made a slashing motion across her neck. Ma June

nodded and told him she wasn't in. Imani turned her attention back to the beauty-shop divas.

"Okay, one o'clock. Whatcha getting?"

"A wash and set."

Imani pointed at the other customer.

"I'm getting a wash and blow-dry, with a deep conditioner."

"You come on, then."

"Why her? I've been here the longest."

Imani explained. "A deep conditioner takes longer and she'll have to sit. I can get her started then go on straight through with you."

"Are these the Bible days or something? The last go first and the first go last? I've been here since one o'clock, and now it's past two-thirty." She looked around Imani. "Shari!"

"Whatcha calling my daughter for?" Ma June asked. "You just said you'd go along with whatever Imani said."

"That's *before* I knew I wasn't gonna like what she decided. Sha-rrrr-A!"

"Ain't you a trip," Imani said, trying to control her temper.

"Look, you ain't nobody but the shampoo girl. Your name is not on the window. Hers is. Sha-rrrr-A!"

Shari yelled without turning around. "Handle it, Imani."

Ma June made a big sound, too big for a laugh but just right for gloating. The bangles on her wrists chimed in too.

One o'clock turned red. "Y'all don't understand. I have a hot date tonight."

"Me too," Two o'clock said.

"Well I have to look extra good. My man drives a Mercy-D."

"So does mine."

Both women faced off now.

"Well my man is a doctor."

"So is mine."

Imani whispered under her breath. *"Oh no."*

The two women felt a wisp of realization. Their eyes bucked.

One o'clock asked, "Gynie?"

"Yeah!"

They both said his name at the same time: "Marvin!"

One o'clock said, "I'm meeting him for a drink after work."

Two o'clock said, "I'm meeting him later on at the club."

Blink-blink. Now it's on. The women jumped back and threw up their fists and started balling. Imani stepped between them. "Stop it!"

"Move!" One o'clock growled. "I'm gonna knock her into next week."

"Naw, baby. I know karate."

"So what? *I know crazy.*"

Imani held them back until Shari moved in to help. She muscled her way between them. "Ladies—and I'm giving the benefit of the doubt when I say ladies—I'm running a class establishment here. So y'all take that mess outside, down the street."

"Right," One o'clock said. "I'm going to take her outside and beat her down like the dog she is."

Imani checked the woman hard. "You got your canines mixed up, sistah. Mr. Marvin is the dog who deserves to get the rolled-up newspaper."

"Right," Ma June said, thumping her silver cane against the floor. "We've got to stop blaming each other when a man mistreats us and messes around. You are responsible for your own happiness. Nobody else. Don't let him use you then turn around and dog the sister who's caught in the middle just like you."

The words were like a referee hollering break. The fighters dropped their hands.

Shari felt sorry for them. "Hey, we've all been there before. Ain't no shame, it's just the game."

One o'clock turned to leave. She reached down and picked up her cup of pop, then whirled around and threw it—ice and all.

Two o'clock was quicker than Venus Williams going after a

drive. She dived behind Imani who got drenched from head to toe with orange pop.

"Dawg," she heard one of the customers in the back say, "she's been crushed. *Orange Crushed.*"

Imani's face was twisted in anger. She lunged forward.

The two women ran out the door. Shari grabbed Imani by the waist and held her back. "Cool down. It's over. Cool down." Imani finally stopped struggling. "Go on and get cleaned up, girl."

Imani went to her locker and wiped down. She looked at herself in the mirror. She'd forgotten to close her smock. Underneath her oversized jersey was stained orange.

"Mirror, mirror on the wall. Which beauty shop has the most drama of them all?"

As if on cue, Shari stuck her head in the room. "Come on, Imani. We gotta get these folks shampooed."

"You got eyes. Look at me, Shari. I need to go home and get changed. I'm a hot mess."

"You're okay. Truth is, I can't spare you that long. I've got two shampoo girls out, and you know Minnie's got everybody backed up. If I don't start moving some of these customers out of here now, I'm going have a riot on my hands."

"I feel sticky."

"Imani, if those customers start leaving that's cold cash walking out the door. I can't afford that. Neither can you. And you *do* wanna get paid on time, don'tcha?"

Imani dropped her head and waved her hand overhead like a sistah feeling it on Sunday morning in the back pew.

"Thanks, girl."

For the rest of the afternoon, it was a game of spin the Imani. Can you do this? Come do that. Ma June left early for a doctor's appointment. She handed Imani three messages from Professor Hopson and told her she might as well help answer the phones, too, since all the calls were for her.

Imani. Imani. Imani.

Her hands throbbed from the hot water that pricked her fingers like thousands of mischievous pins. Her back ached in the small area connecting the tailbone and the spine; ached from lugging boxes of shampoo and from leaning over the bowls, massaging scalps.

The smell of perm made her cough, and she tried not to inhale and breathed through her mouth instead. But after six hours, Imani's throat felt dry and parched, barren. But did that stop her? Not Imani. She kept moving, doing her best. Being it all. Making money to help her dad. Going over Taz's latest track in her head, getting the song down pat. Having the goal of helping everyone else above and beyond the call of duty. But what about Imani? What about what she really needed?

The last customer to leave the shop was a senior citizen who had worked Imani like Kizzy.

The water's too hot.

Now it's too cold.

Can you get me a magazine?

I think I need some dandruff shampoo. How much? Put on a mask and pull out a gun why don'tcha. No thanks.

Can you see if my ride is out there yet?

Can I have some coffee?

Imani just knew she was going to get a nice tip from the woman. But the old lady clutched her purse as she walked towards the door.

"Wait, Imani. I didn't forget about you. You've been good as gold. I'll be right back."

"I have change," Imani offered, fingering the singles in her smock pocket.

But the old lady left anyway. Ten minutes later she came back. "Here," she said, and handed Imani a Happy Meal from McDonald's.

Shari laughed her heart out as she locked the door behind the old woman.

"That ain't funny. You know it's not."

Shari took the hamburger out of the box and tore it in half.

"Whatcha doing, Shari?"

"Splitting the tip."

Imani collapsed into one of the chairs and used her feet to spin around and around. "What a day!"

"Say, who's that professor dude that kept calling today?"

"Just a guy I ran into over at A.U. Ain't nothing happening. I'm not calling him back."

"Good. 'Cause you know them uptown men only want a downtown girl for one thing . . . to get them some *edge-jam-macation between the sheets.*"

"It wasn't like that. He was just talking junk about music, that's all. Trying to convince me that jazz is better than rap."

"Ooooh-wee. Taz would have beat him down for that."

"Ya know *I* did."

"So you honestly blew him off, Imani?"

"Of course. I got too much going on as it is."

"Like trying to wear out my salon chair with all that spinning around you doing?"

"On days like today, Shari, I feel like maybe, just maybe, if I go fast enough, long enough, life will change."

Shari grabbed the chair arm and stopped her friend from spinning. "You okay?"

Silence.

"You hear me?"

Imani kept her head back and her eyes closed.

"Talk to me, girl."

"I'm just worried."

"About what?"

"About this. If this is gonna be it for me. Know what I'm saying? If this is *all.* Because if it is, that's so messed up, I don't know if I'll be able to stand it."

"Why would this be all, Imani? You're working on your music, right?"

"And so are a whole lot of other people."

"But they don't have your talent."

"My mama had talent and she didn't make it."

"But you've got Taz working on your sound."

"My mama had my daddy."

"All right, girl, chill. You're too down on yourself for me. Let's hear it."

"What?"

"Oh, you wanna play stupid now? Break out your mother's song. That melody is a killer. I don't know why you haven't slapped some cold lyrics on that bad boy yet."

"I've tried. But I can't, Shari. I'm just not ready yet."

"Let's hear it, then. We'll both feel better."

Imani concentrated, then found her voice. She hung the notes up like silk gowns in a closet. A rolling tongue shaped the sounds in a smooth scat. Imani felt a slight gurgle in the back of her throat and a tingling in her ears. Releasing the melody from her heart and into the air made the room smaller, a cluster of sound that took up space, that staged pockets of energy at her feet, above her head, up against her sides, beside her cheeks. Her mother's melody, a melody spawned by nature it seemed, how else could it sound so real, like diamonds from the earth, rain from the clouds, hope from the heart?

"That's what I'm talkin' 'bout, Imani." Shari applauded. "This ain't all for you, girl. Don't you worry none. This ain't hardly all."

Chapter Seven

When we want more out of life, sometimes we have to shuffle the cards. Some people take the deck out of life's hands and deal from the bottom.

The arson at Club Maceo was a bottom card.

"What's going on with the insurance people, Taz?" Biggie asked. He was talking on his cell phone as he sped down the highway.

"Man, Biggie. It's early. How come you up and out after all that partying we did with those hos last night?"

"You better hope Imani don't have your phone bugged, player. And I'm up 'cause I'm a businessman. Now what's the holdup with them insurance people?"

"There was that big storm the week before the fire, remember? Right outside of Virginia? Tore up houses and businesses left and right. All the insurance companies are backed up."

"So how much you got for me this time?"

"With what I got from unloading trucks and what Imani gave Maceo, that's almost three hundred. We short a bill."

Biggie silently weighed his options.

Biggie was biggie because at birth he was the spitting image of his father, who had chosen the low road rather than the high road of family. Lovingly, as she lay alone in the hospital room, his mother blessed the boy with his father's name and prayed that he would be a better man.

Time jogged uphill. By the time the boy was five, he was indeed the physical carbon copy of his father except for his hulking size. Relatives said, "Little Mitch is a biggie."

Biggie's body outgrew his baby face but not his heart. Fiercely protective of his mother, June, and sister, Shari, Biggie would do anything for family. Family extended to Taz, whom he met after school one day on the playground, the newest tenant at the foster home down the street. Pitiful-looking and scrawny, Biggie thought that if he took care of this little boy, maybe God would bring his father back to take care of him.

That blessing never came, and Biggie's focus became being the family protector, loyal friend and, later, provider.

"Biggie? You there, man?"

"Yeah I'm here, Taz. Tell you what. I'll drop in a bill this time. I know you'll pay me back when the insurance money comes. But here's what I want you to do: Tell Maceo to get in that insurance company's ass like he's getting in my wallet, understand? 'Cause this can't go on much longer. And that's for real."

Maceo had tried dealing from the bottom of the deck too—a long time ago.

He had faked a recording contract trying to bluff a deal out of a white producer who wanted Mae to sing for him. It was 1972. He'd been playing gigs and coming home to Mae, working on songs he arranged especially for her. They were other folks' songs, but the way Maceo changed the key and the way Mae threw in scats on the hooks, whatever song she sang soon belonged to her and only her.

You can't hide talent. Even if you're riding someone else's coattails or singing their songs. Maceo could arrange his butt off, but he couldn't write original music. He could hear a melody for the first time and right away know where it was going—but come up with it himself, cold? No way.

So when the white producer from Manhattan Sounds came backstage at the little club they were playing in New York and talked about the great writers that he had, Maceo became jealous. The producer was pushy, crowding Mae to find out where she stood. Mae was polite and told him to talk to her man. She knew how to let a king be a king. Unfortunately, it ended up costing her a shot at a real music career.

Maceo faked a contract. He'd gotten it from a friend who worked in the mailroom at CBS records. He got a standard contract and typed in his name and Mae's too. He left the date and their signatures blank. Then Maceo forged the VP's signature on the document.

During the next visit from Manhattan Sounds, Maceo flashed the contract. He told the producer that CBS had made them an offer that included giving him full producing rights. They hadn't signed it yet, Maceo said, because they wanted to know if Manhattan Sounds would match the terms and sweeten it with a little more cash. If so, the talented couple would sign with them.

That was the bottom card.

Maceo dealt from the bottom not for himself, as much as he wanted to succeed, but for his woman. He wanted to protect Mae, keep her from getting pushed around and musically pimped. It wasn't selfish. Maceo wasn't playing the game just for him, it was for his lover and the family he hoped they would one day have together.

What Maceo didn't know was that the producer had worked at CBS records before joining the smaller, lesser-known Manhattan Sounds and knew the signature on the contract was a fake.

He called Maceo on it. Fronted him in a room full of musicians, embarrassed him, thinking Mae would drop him like a hot potato and sign with Manhattan Sounds. But Mae refused. She knew how to let a king be a king because Mae possessed the class of a queen.

Angry and now embarrassed himself, the big-shot producer spread the word that Maceo was a liar and couldn't be trusted. Now he couldn't get work and neither could Mae. They got blackballed. But not every blackball has an eight on it.

When the world is against you, where do you turn? You turn to the love of your life. Maceo and Mae grew closer. They found comfort in each other's arms where before there was only passion. When frustrated, they shared looks that said—through vision and not voice—*I know.* The sound of each other's breathing at night was a steady stroke that made their spirits feel, *it's gonna be okay.*

Maceo took all the money that he had saved and put it into producing a jazz album for Mae. It was called *Songs from the Heart.* A couple of critics liked it, but for the most part it was ignored. Maceo didn't have the clout to get it radio play. Besides, everyone was turning away from jazz and getting into some new diva named Donna Summer.

"Try disco," someone told Maceo.

"*Man, please,*" he replied.

Other musicians envied the couple's defiance at first, but after a while people just began to go on about their business. They didn't see the pride any longer; they saw stubbornness. They didn't see shut doors; they saw losers. Anytime anyone told Mae she should strike out on her own, she turned that person away with a face of steel and a voice of stone. "We'll be all right together."

The couple married and thought the change in dynamics would spark a change in their luck. But luck held a grudge and continued to rub their faces in it. The years began to pass quickly, but the hard times passed slowly. After a while, Maceo finally started landing a job here and there, playing background music for radio commercials. He was right about disco. It had the longevity of a lunar eclipse. But somehow it managed to overshadow the window of opportunity for Maceo's talent.

Times got tougher and tougher. Maceo had to pick up odd jobs as a day laborer or a bartender. Mae would go to the grocery store and come home with so little food that the tan plastic bag would swing from her wrist like a Sunday pocketbook. The only time her belly got full was when she became pregnant with Imani.

"Put your hand here and feel, Maceo."

His shaky palm inched forward through the air like a frightened bird.

"Why are you so scared?"

"I'm not scared. Just excited."

Mae steadied his hand against her stomach. "Feel that? She's going to be a star."

"How can you tell?"

" 'Cause other babies kick and roll all herky-jerky or sit still as stone. My baby girl moves like a river. She's got rhythm."

And the rhythm that new life finds within the womb has pull; like planets in orbit. Mae would sing to Imani before she was born, humming really, so the notes would go deep down inside. That was part of the pull between mother and daughter. When it was time for her to be born, Imani would hardly let go, so comfortable was she surrounded by a womb of sound. Mae labored for twenty-two hours before the doctors induced.

And finally the baby came, sailing out, freckled and cupped like a seashell on its back, washing up on shore. Hollering too.

Imani was born with voice. She lost it three years later when her mother suffered a heart attack while working a double shift cleaning an office building. Maceo had the funeral that weekend and should have asked for a separate coffin for his ambition. He buried it along with his wife. He would never, ever play seriously again.

Imani was weepy for a long time afterwards. She desperately missed the sound of her mother's voice. As the little girl's sadness began to fade, her fondness for music grew. She desired to be different from her mother . . . a singer . . . and her father . . .

a musician. Rap became her music of choice: words and rhymes, messages and music. Taz steered her in that direction too, and she followed along with her father's blessing.

Maceo gave his blessing because Taz loved music with a passion. And when he worked with Imani in the little garage he'd turned into a studio, or at their place on the family piano, Taz packed that passion around her like pillows, cushioning her, guiding her.

Whiskey and growing up were the two things that sometimes became a fence between Maceo and Imani. She became an adult and sometimes wanted to boss the old man around, telling him what to do and what not to do, namely drink. Thank God it wasn't a solid fence, more like a metal one with bars, the kind you can see through, and reach through, even get up and over when you truly want to.

Maceo watched now as Taz went over a song with Imani. He stopped and started the tape, mixed in some piano.

"Listen up, Imani. I want you to rap the hook line over this sample riff I found."

"Hear me out, Taz. The song is slamming. No doubt. But I'm telling you the rhyme I wrote is stronger. It would be the bomb up against this new beat."

"Naw, Imani. Let's just go with what we got."

"Can't you take a look?"

"Later, Imani. Later."

"You always talking about later. How come later never comes. What's up with that?"

"Stop tripping, Imani."

"Stop hating."

"Girl, you wanna argue or you wanna work?"

Maceo chuckled to himself. The two of them together now reminded him of the first time he sat them next to each other on this very same piano.

Now Taz had grown into a man, Imani into a woman, and their dreams into braiding vines that Maceo truly hoped would reach to the sky. That's what he wanted for his daughter: the boundless sky where music had no ceiling, no walls, and no acoustics to shape and limit. He and Mae had been shaped and limited. Surely life would treat his baby fairer.

"Hey son," Maceo said, barging into the room, purposely interrupting, "play one of those slow tunes I showed you back in the day."

"Awww, Maceo."

He playfully grabbed Taz around the neck and faked a choke. "Do like I say."

Taz gave in. "Just one." He began to play a sweet, slow jazz ballad.

Maceo let the notes sink into his soul. "I'm so glad the fire didn't get this old piano. It's got a good sound to it."

"Don't it, though?" Imani agreed. At night sometimes she'd dream that her mother was sitting at this piano, singing. The thought made Imani smile.

"Whatcha smiling about?" Maceo said, grabbing his daughter by the arm. "Come on here and dance, pretty girl."

"Pretty," Taz grumped, "but hardheaded."

"Daddy, he won't look at the lyrics I wrote."

Maceo had Imani by the hand now. "What did I tell you when y'all were kids?"

"Let Taz show me."

"Right." Maceo put his hand around Imani's waist and began to dance. "I remember how quick you learned to dance."

He stepped back and twirled Imani around. Taz played the slow jazzy tune. Maceo gently pulled Imani in, and her smile reminded him of someone special to him, someone lost but not forgotten. He drew Imani close.

"I want so much for you. You just don't know."

"I do know, Daddy," Imani whispered in his ear. "I do."

" 'Member how you used to hate for me to try and dance with you when Shari and the other kids were around? Said I was embarrassing you."

"And you *did*. You big show-off."

"Listen at ya. Tired of the old man already."

"I'll never get tired of dancing with my father."

And they danced.

Taz played and finished off the song with a beautiful twinkling flourish up the scale. He turned around and looked at them, hugging and smiling at each other. A family.

"Can a brother cut in?"

"Hell no!" Maceo barked.

"Ahhh-ha!" Imani teased.

Maceo picked up his horn that lay on top of the piano. "G'on, boy."

And he played for them. Taz and Imani. *Maceo really played for them.* But most of all, he hoped for them.

Chapter Eight

Shari was a hopeless chatterbox. Words were her calling card. She asked deep questions, silly questions, quoted philosophy, tried to fashion herself into a highfalutin' lady, but cussed like a pimped player when she was mad. But most of all, she loved to say controversial stuff in the beauty shop, especially stuff she knew Ma June wouldn't like and would want to debate. It was a boring afternoon. Shari wanted to shake things up a little bit. Make that *a lot.*

"Hey, y'all," she called out. "I wonder if Coretta Scott King has been getting any since Martin died."

Ma June was right on it. "Oh no, you didn't go there. I don't care what these men say up in the barbershop. Sistahs in the beauty shop are supposed to have respect."

"C'mon, Ma. I'm just throwing it out there for conversation's sake."

"Still it's disrespectful. Coretta is the first lady of the civil rights movement."

"So? The civil rights movement can't keep her back warm at night. She's a woman like any other woman. She wants to be loved."

"We love Coretta. All the sistahs in the world love her for the way she kept Martin's legacy alive. Plus she raised those four kids all by herself and not a lick of trouble out of any one of them."

"But Ma, be real. Coretta was a young woman when her husband was gunned down. She still had to wanna go out and kick it sometimes."

"What? Coretta stepping out in the club doing the twist? I don't think so."

"What about the electric slide?"

"Quit it, Shari."

"Okay. You right, Mama. Black folks wouldah lost their nappy-head minds if she was out there getting her groove on with some cutie in the club. Coretta was not hanging out."

"Thank goodness. Now you're talking like you've got some sense."

"Yep, she couldn't roll like that. Not in public. Too common. Nope, Coretta was creeping."

"Shari, don't make me send you outside for a switch."

"Ma, don't be so touchy. Coretta is human. She's flesh and blood. Y'all don't wanna let her be a woman. That's why she's on love lockdown. 'Cause all y'all old-school folks don't want her to have a life."

"Coretta don't need a life. She has a role."

"What's her role?"

"When racist stuff jumps off, Coretta comes forward and tells us what Martin would have done. Her role is not to be making booty calls in the middle of the night."

"Stop, Ma. I didn't make it all nasty like that. Like she's rolling around with some bum. But why can't she keep company—a judge or bank president—have a little something-something on the side? I mean, she's been a widow for years. Have you ever seen Coretta with a male escort?"

"No."

"Jackie Kennedy had more than one."

"Black folks can't get away with the stuff that white folks can, Shari."

"Except for O. J."

"You wrong for that. O. J. did not kill those people."

"Forget O. J. for a minute, Ma."

"Naw, forget him forever. Back to Coretta. She's escorting a legacy. Our children need to see how a woman of history, of status, of sophistication should carry herself. Jackie Kennedy found someone else to marry, and her business was all in the tabloids. That mess threw a shadow on Camelot."

"Meaning what, Ma?"

"Meaning Coretta is escorting our Camelot and that image of a woman dedicated to her husband and her children *no matter what* is the kind of example that we as black people need. And must keep. Coretta is a lady. Do you understand?"

"Yes."

"Now will you please shut up about Coretta? Don't ask no more stupid-ass questions about Coretta."

"Yes, ma'am. Can I ask another question, though?"

"Is it about Coretta?"

"No, it is not."

"Go 'head, baby."

"Have you ever seen Rosa Parks with a man?"

All the ladies in the beauty shop yelled, "Don't go there!"

Suddenly the door opened and everyone looked up. Professor Hopson stood there. "Hello, ladies."

"Hello," they all said back like a choir.

Hopson felt a little embarrassed as the women, young and old, openly checked him out.

"Can I help you, baby?" Ma June asked.

"Yes. I'm looking for Imani."

"And you are?"

"Professor Orenthal Hopson."

"What you say!" Ma June thumped the floor twice with her

cane. "So you're the one making Ma Bell rich calling up here looking for Imani."

Professor Hopson smiled.

"I'll get her for you. Have a seat."

Hopson stood. He didn't want to lose the edge he needed to argue Imani down and convince her to come to the university and work with him. He wanted to win that bet.

"Imani, you've got a guest out front. A cute guest."

"Who, Ma June?"

"That professor. He's young too . . . looks too young to be a college professor."

Imani walked to the doorway and peeked out. "Dog, he's hardheaded. I've been blowing him off like crazy and he still won't give up."

"I like it in him. Go talk to the man."

"Ma June, he wants me to work for him at the university, be a jazz singer. I'm not trying to hear that. I'm a rapper."

"Like it's gonna kill you to learn something new?"

Shari came to the back. "So that's him, huh? He's corny but cute as pie."

"I told him I wasn't interested."

"Good for you, girl. Taz is hooking up your sound." Shari gave Imani a high five. "Later for him."

"Well you tell the boy, then," Ma June huffed. "I've been lying so much I don't know whether I'm coming or going. So you do it, Imani. Stop running if you don't wanna be bothered; be a woman and tell the man where to get off. If I was ten years younger you could tell him to get off at my house."

Imani and Shari laughed. Imani smirked. "Ten years?"

"Shut up, you. Go'n, Imani. And take him outside so all these hot-curling hussies up in here won't be in your business."

Imani took Hopson outside. He started talking hard and fast. "I've been calling you and calling you."

"I got the messages."

"So are you just rude, or are you just stubborn?"

"Maybe both," she sassed. "Can't you take no for an answer, or are you just like one them pain in the ass brothahs we got around here in the 'hood?"

"Maybe both," he sassed back. "Imani, I'm offering you a great opportunity. What are you afraid of?"

"Who said I'm afraid?"

"Me."

"And what am I supposed to be scared of . . . yo' ass?"

"Yes. Because I'd work you like you've never been worked before. I'd bring out talent in you that you didn't even know you had. You're right, Imani. You should be scared. I'd be scared of me too."

"Hops, I ain't afraid of nothing and nobody. *Especially* some uptown professor with nothing else to do but chase me down like the law."

"How can I convince you?"

"You can't. Now I gotta get back to work. Stop calling."

"Then I'll come by."

"Hops, this is a place of business. You can't be hanging around here. I gotta get back to work. You costin' me money, man."

Professor Hopson took his card out of his pocket and gave it to Imani. "Then call me. I want you to work for me and at the same time we'll work on your music too. This is important."

Imani found herself mad and flattered at the same time. "Why?" She snatched the card. "Why is it so damn important?"

The bet flashed through Hopson's mind. But he answered, "Because I hate to see talent wasted."

"Then go find you a charity case. Ain't none here." Imani opened the door. "But thanks just the same. I 'preciate it."

"You didn't throw away my card this time. That's progress."

"That's Do Not Litter." But he was right. She didn't throw

the card away. Imani went back into the shop. "Bye." She walked slow and put some dip in her hip so he could see all the glory of her leaving. After all, Imani was a woman, wasn't she?

And some women just love to show off their stuff to a man—especially the hoochie kind. Like the hoochie who was ready to perform that night for Taz, Biggie, and the boys.

"Give me a chance, Taz. Just keep your eyes on me."

Taz, Biggie, and two of his strong-arm boys were all sitting on the couch in an abandoned storage house that Taz had turned into a tiny music studio.

This wanna-be, wish-she-had-talent, more-brass-than-class, five-feet-eight-in-three-inch-spikes half groupie, half harlot stood wide-legged on the table.

"She's gonna jack up the furniture," one of Biggie's boys said.

"We'll eat on the floor," Biggie deadpanned, leering at the woman's breasts.

Like the Grinch who had a heart two sizes too small, this hoochie had a top two sizes too small and no heart at all. She knew Taz was Imani's man, and she was out to steal him. "Like I said, keep your eyes on me, Taz. I got Imani beat, baby. I can dance and rap too."

Taz and the woman were locked in a visual tango. She twirled her head slightly and licked her lips. Taz turned his head slightly then used his index finger to stir the air.

Like a puppet attached to a string, she rotated around, an invisible hula-hoop kept up by her whirling hips.

"What you see is what you get," she said in a sexy voice.

"When?" Biggie jumped up clowning. "When?"

"I'm talking to Taz, Biggie."

"Baby, we the musketeers. One for all and all for a piece of ass."

The men started laughing and slapping five, all except Taz.

"They're ignorant," he said to soothe the woman's anger.

"I know."

"You do have a marketable look." Taz tried to sound super-professional, like the men who voiced-over the BMW commercials.

"Huh?" One of Biggie's boys turned to him. "What's he talking about, Biggie?"

"Don't y'all know nothin'? That's producer lingo, dog. That means, 'Damn baby, your body is booming.' "

The woman on the table bent over from the waist. "So whatcha gonna do for me, Mister Producer Man?"

"I can think of a couple of things we can do in the studio."

"A couple!" One of Biggie's boys laughed. "I can think of a hundred!"

"Sssh!" Taz frowned at the other guys. He turned his attention back to the woman on the table. "You know a performer has to be ready to throw down at anytime, in front of anybody. Do you think you can showcase your talents now?"

The boys looked at Biggie. He translated: " 'Woman, g'on and shake ya ass.' "

They began to bark like dogs.

"Let's get busy," Biggie demanded. He flipped on the boom box at his feet. A CD that Taz had produced was in it. The male rapper's voice violated the room. "This boy is the bomb. Taz hooked him up with the remix. G'on, woman, groove with it."

The woman started to dance. Body language is a monster. What engulfs the mind the body mirrors. Hesitation is found in a stutter step. Disbelief is found in raised eyebrows. Anger is found in flailing arms. Sexiness is found in the sway of the hips. That was how the dance started.

But then it took a nasty turn.

Raunchiness is when those hips swing like a pendulum, not caring what the danger. Swaying back and forth, just laying to cut into the promises of *only you, baby* that couples like Imani and Taz make to each other. Swaying to make a deep cut, to slice open what they shared; to watch it bleed out and wonder if any of it can be saved.

Body language is a monster.

The dancer used moves from street hos to ancient history. She strutted and stalked like the ladies of the night trying to trade lying on their backs for folding greenbacks. She swiveled and bobbed up and down like the harem girls trying to find favor with the king.

She came down from the table the way the snake slithered down the tree in the Garden of Eden. And instead of spiraling at Adam's feet, this woman straddled Taz's body as he sat, bumping and grinding as hard and as fast as she could.

Biggie howled, *"That ain't rap. That's lap!"*

Body language is a monster.

Remember? *Hesitation is found in a stutter step,* like now as Imani paused in the doorway thinking it strange that the music was so loud. *Disbelief is found in raised eyebrows* like now as she stood in the doorway watching Taz get rocked by a rump-shaker relationship breaker. *Anger is found in flailing arms . . .* like now as Imani tried to scratch the woman blind, snatch her bald, and knock her silly . . . like now as she kept Taz's lying arms at bay.

"C'mere, baby. Imani. C'mere. I wanna talk to you, baby."

Imani's body ran. Her legs ran until they carried her to Shari's house where she had been staying since the fire. Her tears ran until her hurt feelings turned into angry pride. Her mind ran around in circles as she desperately tried to figure out what to do.

She plopped on the cot that was now her bed; a stack of unpaid bills and her bag flopped onto the floor. A card fell out. Imani picked it up, an occasional tear wetting the corners. She thumped it with her index finger, reached for her cell, and dialed. The answering machine on the other end clicked on. Imani cleared her throat and got ready for the beep. "Hello, Hops? This is Imani. Remember you told me to call? I'm ready to work something out."

Chapter Nine

The next morning Imani was ready to work something out in *her world, her way* while Biggie was working things out in *his world, his way* for Mr. Watson, the man he strong-armed for.

Biggie's fierce nature and loyalty had caught the eye of the neighborhood loan shark many years ago. In the fairy tale *Pinocchio*, Geppetto made a boy out of wood. Mr. Watson was a ghetto Geppetto. He made a gangsta out of a boy. But in truth, Biggie could be more reasonable than ruthless, more humane than hard, more Robin Hood than Gotti.

That was Biggie's character, and for some reason Mr. Watson liked that. He hoped that that kind of character was in the son his ex-wife began turning against him at age ten. His son was now a grown man who wouldn't have anything to do with him.

Mr. Watson used a car wash as a front. He, Biggie, and another senior enforcer named Claude were there now handling business. They were in the dark storage room with its gray concrete walls. This was the message center, where those who owed but hadn't paid were dialed up and beat down by Biggie and Claude. It was Biggie's turn to carry out the orders to hammer down and intimidate.

"I tried to cut you some slack but naw, you gotta get your ass kicked!" Biggie yelled at the frightened man hunched on the floor. "What's up with that, huh?"

A naked high-watt bulb swinging overhead added to the circus-of-horror atmosphere in the room. Mr. Watson sat back in his five-hundred-dollar dark blue suit and two-hundred-dollar tassel shoes, watching quietly, thoughtfully. He played with a gold medallion he kept on a gold chain that was linked to his pocket. Mr. Watson was a clean-shaven man, unlike the television crime characters on *NYPD Blue,* those stereotypical nefarious Negroes who are lawless for little or nothing. He had built an empire over the years. Mr. Watson reasoned now with this dubious debtor sprawled at his heels.

"Man, you know what disturbs me the most? You haven't been delivering the mail because you're too scared to show your face around here. You've got everybody in the neighborhood mad at me."

"I'm sorry!"

Claude stepped forward. "You whining?"

Claude loved to inflict pain; always wanted to hurt someone, see him or her bleed. An anthropologist of contemporary street life would find him to be *the missing link.* Claude's body was almost too big to be human and oddly shaped with an oblong head and Spock ears. He had a beastly attitude too, but lacked the fairness that animals in the jungle rule by.

Biggie blocked Claude with his back. He began acting overzealous in his mission to maul this welcher who whined on the floor at their feet. That's because to Biggie, he was still a man. Biggie knew Claude would hurt and humiliate him beyond reason just for the fun of it. And this was no sadistic game to Biggie, it was strictly business.

"He's mine!" Biggie yelled into the mailman's face. Then he whispered to him, *"Cover up."*

The mailman became a caterpillar personified. He curled his body up into a tight ball.

Biggie kicked him hard; the sound of boot thrashing against flesh had a crippling ring to it.

"Oh God," the mailman moaned.

"God hands out blessings," Mr. Watson pointed out. "Call on somebody who can hand you some goddamn money. You owe me five thousand dollars and counting."

Biggie grabbed the mailman by the shirt and slapped him across the mouth. Next Biggie grabbed his arm but Mr. Watson stopped him.

"Don't mess up his hands, Biggie. He's got to deliver the mail. It's check day tomorrow. I don't want the old ladies in the neighborhood hollering at me."

Biggie yanked the mailman up by the shoulders instead, slapping him hard across the face once more.

"Oh!" the mailman moaned and pleaded to Mr. Watson. "Mercy, mercy me."

"How'd you know I was a big Marvin Gaye fan? Tell you what. I'm going to give you one more week. Then I want my money, all of it. Can you handle that?"

The mailman's eyes widened at the prospect of being freed from Biggie's clutches.

Biggie leaned into the man's face. "You can see the light at the end of the tunnel, can'tcha now, brah?"

The mailman nodded yes.

"But know this: If you don't come up with that money, that light is going to be me, Biggie the freight train, coming to run your ass over. Feeling me?"

"Oh he's felt you, Biggie," Mr. Watson remarked casually. "More than he ever wanted to."

Biggie marched the mailman to the back door. He spoke low. "Man, get that money or get on 'way from here till you do. Next time it might be Claude."

The mailman limped down the alley.

"Biggie, you sure are softhearted," Claude remarked, pulling up a chair, straddling it backwards.

"Niggah what?"

"You heard me, Biggie."

Mr. Watson spoke up. "I don't know, Claude. Biggie did a good job to me."

"Damn right, I did."

"Not really, Biggie. I'd ah cut him."

"That's why you're Claude and I'm Biggie. Two different men. Two different ways. My debtors are walking around trying to get paid so they can get out from under. Your debtors are in ward six or six feet under."

"Biggie's right, Claude. He does collect faster than you."

"Oh yeah, Mr. Watson? Then where's Maceo's money? Huh? What about that?"

"Claude has a point, Biggie."

"Mr. Watson, like I told you before, that money's coming with all the interest. Because of that fire at Club Maceo there'll be a fat insurance check on the way."

"I've been meaning to ask," Claude questioned, "did you torch the joint?"

Biggie glared at him but said nothing.

"Biggie's too smart to admit to anything," Mr. Watson said admiringly. "My compliments, though. A fire was good thinking."

"Soft thinking if you asked me." Claude sneered before spitting. "He didn't want to kick Maceo's ass 'cause his boy is banging Maceo's daughter."

Biggie shrugged then whipped around. He coldcocked Claude, knocking him out of the chair, across the floor, and up against the concrete wall. "Listen here, you bad body bastard. Stay out of my business."

Claude dabbed at the blood trickling down his chin from his busted upper lip. He relished it like an urban vampire. He reached in his pocket and flicked out a switchblade seven inches long.

Mr. Watson was slightly amused. "My boys, my boys. You cats have one crazy competitive streak between y'all."

Claude squared his shoulders, hunched over, and began stalking forward.

"Put that knife away," Mr. Watson ordered. "Right now."

Claude ignored the demand, and Biggie didn't back down either.

"Claude? Did you hear me? I paid for those clothes on your back and the crib where you live. Don't make me get up out of this chair and get my hands dirty kicking your ass."

Claude sighed. He closed the blade, slipped it into his pocket, and walked out the door, glaring at Biggie all the while.

"Punk," Biggie laughed after he left.

"Biggie, you're tough and you're smart. You're more of a son to me than my very own flesh and blood."

"I know that, Mr. Watson."

"Good. So let me give you one important piece of advice, Biggie."

"Okay."

"Fight a man because he owes you money. Cut him high if he talks about your mama, cut him low if you catch him in bed with your woman. But never ever hit a man because he tells you the truth."

If truth were sight, most people would be either nearsighted, farsighted, cockeyed, or blind. Few would have 20/20 vision. And only the truly blessed would have hindsight.

Hopson's world was now a blur.

It was morning after a restless night. Hopson was shirtless, wearing only wrinkled pajama bottoms. He sat in the house that the university provided for the Ellington Fellow. It was rich with history, from the oil paintings on the walls to the sculptures in the foyer to the interior design by one of the first African-American architects recognized for excellence by the Smithsonian.

By the world's yardstick, Hopson should be overjoyed at his position and his surroundings. An up-and-coming scholar heralded in journals for his research, exalted for his musical talent, loving his craft, but still missing something inside.

Hopson leaned back and propped his bare feet against the mahogany cocktail table, fingering the horn that lay comfortingly across his chest.

Two years ago, a lover's head lay there.

Pressure comes in all forms. What is gravity but the universe's pressure to hold everything down? Hopson's gravity was his family.

They were new black money now, which carries with it the perceived burden of exalted status. Hopson's great-grandfather Leroy had worked in the lab where George Washington Carver discovered nearly infinite uses for the peanut. Although a cleanup man, he helped and learned from Dr. Carver. Because he had a family to support, he was never able to go forward to college and get a degree to become a professor like his mentor. Leroy Hopson had a passionate heart for research but a poor head for finances. He died with no money in the bank.

He did pass along to his son, Junior, a unique recipe for a spicy peanut oil and the hope that his son would one day be a famous professor like he had failed to be. Junior started college with the burning desire to fulfill the legacy of the family's dream.

But it wound up being a dream deferred.

Junior's finances dried up, and he fell madly in love and started a family. He worked forty years in a packaging plant. His son, Hamilton, worked there as well, trying to save money for college, but he too fell in love and never graduated.

Once again, the family dream was deferred.

One day when Hamilton's wife was pregnant with Orenthal's older sister, he remembered the family recipe for spicy peanut oil. His wife and her family, neighbors, church folk, too, raved about the wonderful seasoning. He used it to start a business that he named after the man who first dreamed their dream. Today Leroy Oil is a million-dollar company.

So by the time Orenthal was born, the family had all the goods and a measure of wealth that was growing. When black folks get some money, they set the baby's place with a silver spoon, knife, *and* fork. His father also passed along to Orenthal the dream of having a noted college professor in the family. With Orenthal's gift of music, his family immediately pushed him in that direction. It's easy to stay on course when you're carrying the dreams of past generations. You haven't the strength or the spirit to seek your own road.

Restless overnight after being turned down by Imani, Hopson got up and went into the kitchen for his morning herbal tea. He hopped up onto the counter. Soon the pot-boiling heat of the stove seeped into the countertop and warmed the legs of his pajamas. Letting his heels tap against the bottom kitchen cabinet, Hopson began to daydream.

He thought of his lost love Serena and what she had meant in his life. Sometimes Serena's memory would cruise through his veins like a shot of penicillin, disabling anything that could disease his body with sadness.

The two of them had been careless lovers who sought only the satisfaction of what flesh against flesh could bring. Their passion rotated on an axis of *all night long* and spun on the abandon of *whenever*.

When we are reckless with our emotions, someone is bound to get wrecked. So Serena asked him if he loved her and being so young, so cautious, so trained, instead of saying the answer that beat inside his chest, he measured.

Well, Hopson had thought, didn't he savor the taste of her skin against his tongue? Didn't he want to be with Serena more than anyone else he'd ever dated? But didn't she personify what his father had termed a trap? A young, overwhelming love that could jack up his soul and derail his professional dreams? One just like that, which had caught and bottled the family dream and shelved it for past generations of Hopson men?

The basis of all music is science, the root and the square of it. But Hopson had been groomed so much towards academic success that his emotional self was learning disabled.

Serena would have had to be a behavioral science major—and willing to put in the extra hours to get a PhD in romance—to figure it out. But she too was young, yet not strung out on goals and pedigrees, so all she had desired was an answer that would make her catch her breath; like she did when he hit a high note on the horn or hit her spot between the sheets.

What Hopson did not understand in life, but what he could in music, was the power of the hook. He didn't give Serena what she needed, *so she couldn't give him what he needed.* They were out of tune with each other and couldn't hook up right. Their song of selves had no balance.

So, measure for measure, the answer to her question was *I'm not sure.*

And "I'm not sure" will sink a love life quicker than that iceberg that sunk the *Titanic.*

And it was the speed by which they left each other in fear of what was needed to get them to that special place that left them both emotionally paralyzed.

How could Hopson begin to rehab his romantic soul? How could Hopson achieve an ancestor's dream and still fill the longing of his own heart?

Little did he know that just as sure as the kitchen kettle's whistle told him it was time for tea, fate, too, would have a sound for him. That sound would signal that it was time for a change when he played the message on his voice mail at the office later that afternoon. The message began . . . *"Hello Hops? This is Imani. Remember you told me to call?"*

Chapter Ten

And just as Hopson would have no problem remembering when he played the message, Imani had no problem remembering that she was a performer and that for a performer, the show, despite all drama, must go on.

"Ladies, ladies . . . ladies . . . Welcome to Shari's House of Style! I'm Imani. I'm your hip-hop hostess for the evening."

Imani wore a black catsuit with a speckled gold-and-black head wrap, large hoop earrings, and sling-back pumps. Shari had on the same outfit. She was standing in the rear of the shop, behind a crowd of loyal customers.

Imani was providing the commentary for this annual event despite her aching heart. She was determined to be a trooper for Shari.

Shari liked to treat her best customers to dinner and a male model fashion show at the salon. Each year the women got progressively wilder. Each year the models wore less and less clothing.

"As your hostess for the evening, I'm gonna be speaking to y'all from the heart. Here at Shari's House of Style it's all about you. Hey, didn't y'all get your grub on? Wasn't that a slamming buffet? Who had the cake? Wasn't it off the hook?"

"Yeah," a heavyset woman in the front row yelled. "We had the pound cake, now bring on the beefcake!"

All the women began to cheer.

Imani laughed. "Hold on."

"I plan to hold on," a sharply dressed woman cackled. "I plan to hold on to the first fine man that comes walking down that aisle!" Then she took off her glasses.

"Why'd you take your glasses off?" Imani asked.

"I wanna make sure I grab the wrong thing by mistake!"

Everyone howled.

"I hate to say it," Imani said with a grin, "but *I'm supposed to tell y'all to relax and kick back."*

Ma June yelled out, "You ain't said nothing but a word, baby girl!" She jabbed the air with her cane. "I can't kick no more, but I sure can lick!"

"Tacky old broad," one of the customers whispered to her girlfriend.

"Ssshh! You know that's *Shari's mama!"*

Imani continued, *"I'm also supposed to tell y'all to feel free to let your hair down."*

Shari yelled, "And don't worry. If your curls fall flat, I'll bump up the ends. If your weave falls out, I'll stitch it back in!"

The ladies gave each other a high five.

"Yeah, but how are you going to fix it, Shari, if our husbands catch us with one of those fine male models later on?"

"I'll give you Johnnie Cochran's phone number and Iyanla Vanzant's book, *In the Meantime . . ."*

The ladies cackled and howled; two jumped up and started doing the bump. Sad as Imani was, she felt these crazy women uplifting her spirit.

"Ladies, are y'all ready to have the time of your lives?!"

"Yes we are, Imani!" they shouted.

"All right . . . coming up. We have the mean jean scene. These brothers are gonna be modeling the best bottoms around.

And what better sounds for them to step off to than that old Ohio Players tune . . . 'Skin Tight!' "

The hulking tin jukebox with its speckled red, blue, and green flashing lights began pumping out the sounds; a driving bass line crawled under the floorboards and pounded out a sledgehammering beat.

All the gals started rocking back and forth in their seats, hands went flying in the air, and heads began bobbing up and down.

From a curtained-off area in the rear, the first model walked out. He was slim and towering, body glistening with glitter like a rainbow had wrapped itself around his waist. Designer denim stretched itself across every rock-hard place; the double-stitched seams were hanging on for dear life. If bottled, the man's flawless skin tone would put Coppertone out of business. Muscles rippled all along his bare back as he stopped and posed like some Greek god who was birthed by some African queen. *Body by Zeus. Fine by Cleopatra.* He and every other male model behind him was a ghetto runway superstar.

As for the crowd? Well, let's just say that real women have *curves and nerve.*

One of the women on the aisle stopped the man in midstep. Her hips started doing the tilt-a-whirl boogie. Then she agreed with R. Kelly that ain't nothing wrong with a little bump and grind.

"Awww, to the beat y'all!" Imani boogied her own self. "You go, girl!"

Outside the beauty salon, Biggie and Taz parked and walked up. Taz slyly peeped through the window, finding a sliver of view unblocked by the drawn shades.

"She's in there, Biggie."

"I already told you that. How come you gotta peep in there like Undercover Brother? Go on inside and talk to the woman."

"Biggie, there's a whole bunch of females in there."

"So?"

"So you gonna back me up?"

"You scared of a bunch of women? Move." Biggie barreled forward and looked in. "Damn, player, they do look kindah strong, huh?"

"That's what I'm saying. So you going in with me?"

"I don't know, Taz. I ain't hit a girl since second grade. And 'tween me and you, she kicked my butt!"

"Who, Shari?"

Biggie mused. "Naw." He pointed sheepishly. "Homegirl, third row from the back."

Taz's jaw dropped as he craned his neck trying to see. Biggie slapped him on the back of the neck like he was swatting a fly. "Man, what? Can't you tell I'm just playing?"

Taz rubbed his sore neck. "Time out for playing. Come in with me."

"Okay. But you can't go in there acting weak. You gotta go in there strong." Biggie flexed like the Hulk. "Strong like . . . grrrrrrrrh!"

"Man, please."

Biggie grabbed Taz by the shoulder. "Who got two girlies waiting back at the crib, and who's standing outside looking crazy?"

Taz thought, then growled like Biggie.

"Yeah, that's my dog. G'on in there and get your woman in check."

Taz turned, hesitated, and then turned back around. "How about you go in first?"

"Naw, you go in first."

"No you, Biggie."

"It's your girlfriend."

"It's your sister's salon."

Biggie rubbed his jaw. "Okay. We'll go in together big and bold, just like in the movie *Bad Boys.*"

"Oh yeah," Taz said, building up some courage. "Will Smith and Martin Lawrence. That's us."

"I'm Will Smith."

"At close to three hundred pounds, Biggie, how you gonna be Will Smith?"

" 'Cause I wanna get with fine-ass Jada. I know she's gotten rid of that nappy satellite hairdo she wore in *Matrix Reloaded*. Besides, you know you can be silly as hell sometimes—and who else is that but Martin Lawrence?"

"Aww, Biggie man. Stop ragging on me."

"Then handle business, player. Let's do this."

"Ah'right. On three, we're going in. Count it down, brah."

"One . . . two . . ."—Biggie lunged forward—"three!"

Taz lunged, flicked the knob, and threw his hip against the door.

Biggie pivoted on his back foot, swung back out of the way, and hid on the side of the building.

Taz was inside and heard the door slam behind him. All eyes turned towards him, and the entire place went silent. Imani looked at Taz long and hard. She'd been making a valiant effort to hide her aching heart. But now the sight of Taz made her throat clinch.

"Imani," Taz grunted. Then he began walking towards the front of the salon. "I've been trying to get a hold of you for I don't know how long."

"Do you hear that bass in his voice?" one of the women said to the crowd. *"I know he's not putting bass in his voice."*

"Imani!"

And when the pain of the heart is so fresh, the slightest bit of pressure will open the wound and send gushing forth all manner of disease . . . like hurt, shattered loyalty, and suppressed desire.

As bravely as she had entertained, as much as she knew the show must go on, Imani just as easily began to cry. Two tears fell. Imani turned and ran to the back.

"Wait!" Shari called after her. Shari's mother hobbled forward on her cane. "Get her, Shari." She whacked Taz with her cane when she walked by. "Move outta the way, you bony Romeo."

Shari and Ma June followed Imani to the back. Taz walked forward, really wanting to comfort her. As he got closer to the back, the crowd circled around him, cutting him off.

"Wait a minute. Y'all got it wrong."

Biggie was peeping inside, laughing his guts out.

Someone snapped Taz with a white towel. "Ouch!" Someone else threw some of those hard, plastic rollers at him. "Ouch! That hurt."

Taz jumped up on one of those hefty black chairs connected to a big oval drier and tried to curl around it. "Y'all gone crazy or what?"

"Shut up, you dirty dog!"

"Hold up! Hold up!"

Biggie was watching and laughing. Finally he thought, *I better save him.* He opened the door and stepped into the salon.

Suddenly, all eyes and all weapons *were now on him.*

An angry woman was holding a hair drier like it was an Uzi. She was the interrogator. "Friend of yours, Biggie?"

Biggie looked at the cold stares. Out of the corner of his eye, he could see Taz's pleading eyes and ignored them. "Naw, I don't know that niggah."

"C'mon, Biggie."

"Hey-hey, player. Don't get familiar. You don't know me!" Biggie yelled at Taz then cocked his head and spoke sweetly to the ladies. "What'd he do to make y'all so mad?"

"He made Imani cry!"

"What you say?" Biggie paused for drama. "Ladies, don't worry. I'm gonna make him pay."

"We got it covered!" a woman assured, waving her white towel overhead like a whip.

"But you don't wanna mess up your hair and nails, and stuff like that. Not on this punk. He's not worth it. I'll take him outside and beat him down right for y'all."

Biggie walked forward and grabbed Taz by the shoulders. Taz was confused and let Biggie know it.

"Man, what's up with you?"

"Quiet," he whispered. "I'm trying to save your life."

Biggie began to drag Taz out. Suddenly one of the women standing at Shari's workstation glanced down. A framed photo caught her eye. It was Biggie and Taz locked arm in arm, holding beers.

Vengeful hands raised the photo high in the air so everyone else could see. The angry ladies looked at the photo then at the two men trying to escape.

"Charge!" was their battle cry.

Biggie and Taz took off with the women trailing behind them out into the street.

In the back of the salon, Imani let her tears fall unashamedly in front of the two women she loved dearly and who dearly loved her. She choked back the salty drops long enough to explain her sorrow. "I'm tired of trying to have something special and always having to worry about someone else being disrespectful and cheap enough to try to steal it. Shari, I told you what Taz was doing."

"Yeah."

"What happened?" Ma June asked.

Shari told the story. Ma June sucked wind.

"That's a low-down dirty shame. But y'all oughtah know how these men are by now, don't you?"

"Mama, please don't start preaching."

"Did I ask to be in this pulpit? Don't I wish I wasn't sanctified in heartbreak? It's a sorry fact of life, baby, that these men out here will treat you any old kind of a way if you let 'em. Imani, you might as well just leave that boy alone. If I were in your pumps? I wouldn't be with Taz if he were the last Gilligan on the island."

"That's easy for you to say."

"Girl, what am I?" Ma June asked. "Some angel of love's holiday? No ma'am, Miss Imani. I'm you and Shari's future."

"Mama, please."

"Hush up, Shari. You know your mama knows how to handle the truth. It's got my fingerprints all over it."

Imani sniffed. "Then what's the truth?"

"That black women put their love first and the man's best interest before their own. We let them do what they want to do, and how they want to do, then get all bent out of shape when their plans don't include us."

"We can't make them act right, Mama."

Ma June rubbernecked with each staccato word. "No-we-can-not." Then she softened. "But we can start putting ourselves first. We can start putting our wants and desires first. Why be so inclusive of them when they're not trying to include you?"

By now Imani had dried her eyes. She and Shari both were fixated on the woman advising them. Before now? Really, and truly, they had viewed this older woman as, well, kind of comical. Age had snatched her youth and ran away with it, forcing her to chase it in public like it was a windblown hat. Until now Imani thought that Shari's mama was going through some kind of a phase. That she was trying so hard to dress and act young that she often came off as a frantic, silly caricature of what she once was. Imani realized now that this seasoned woman was real.

"Shari, you mine. And Imani, you *just like* one of mine. I'm telling y'all both something you need to know."

"Tell it, Mama."

"Black women need to fight for their own happiness and hold that up high first. Imani, take some time, step back from Taz, and do something you need to do for you. Understand?"

*   *   *

While Ma June was trying to help the young women understand, Hopson was overjoyed that Imani had changed her mind about coming to work with him at the university.

He hit the repeat button on his office machine.

Imani's voice was music to his ears. *I have a chance,* he thought, *to show Perkins and Sherman both. A real chance to lay those brothers out.*

He hit the replay button again.

This time Hopson got so excited that he started to hum a little tune off the top of his head; a joyous, jazzy refrain: *"Lay those brothers out, yeah!"*

He spun around and spotted a broom propped up against the file cabinet, an oversight by the elderly janitor, Rome.

"Come on. I need a dance partner."

Hopson grabbed the broom and flipped it bristle side up. Gazing at his new partner, he asked, "Bad hair day?"

Hopson smiled.

"Don't be shy. You still look good to me. You have a beautiful brown body and—"

He spun the broom in his hands.

"—you're so graceful on the dance floor—"

Then Hopson dipped his partner.

"—and you don't mind letting a man sweep you off your feet."

Hopson hummed and danced on; his joy became a time chariot that he drove relentlessly. He was propelled to a bygone space kept current in the corner of precious memories.

Hopson pictured his maternal grandparents in one of their quiet times. A child in PJs, he had no sense of privacy, but he had enough sense to know to hide his presence, or what he was about to witness would certainly change.

Ten years old and sleepless, a chest burning from Vicks salve and a throat tickly with phlegm, the sound of his breathing was like the soft downbeat on a slow jam.

"Get the Temps." Granddaddy made the request as he un-screwed lightbulbs in the basement.

Grandma was on her knees flipping through the LPs. "Here they are."

She found the LP just as the room died black then found new life from yellow party bulbs. Their light was soft and runny like the inside of an uncooked egg.

"He asleep, Rose?"

Hopson knew "he" was himself. The little boy drew his legs tightly against his chest, wishing every part of him were invisible but his eyes.

"Yes, Lord."

"Have mercy, woman!"

Granddaddy began dipping his hips and dragging his left leg across the wood floor like the handicapped man who shook a white paper cup and begged for quarters at the corner store. That man looked sad. Granddaddy looked happy.

He swayed and dipped with his arms cupped around his imaginary dance partner, working his hips and rolling his shoulders.

His moves kept Grandma's attention afloat like a leaf on a pond; she *smiled, smiled, and smiled some more.*

"C'mon, woman. Cut in."

She shook her head no. "Keep going. I like seeing what I'm going to get before I get it."

Granddaddy's double step and double sigh, *"Yes-yes,"* whirled around the room upsetting the curtains and creaking the floorboards.

He stutter-stepped over to the love of his life and swept her into his arms and began to dance. "Wait, silly." She giggled. "I haven't put the music on yet."

"No need, baby . . . You're my song."

And she melted into his arms and they danced silently cheek to cheek.

Hopson duplicated the moves now, slow spin, dip, two steps back.

Inside his head, Hopson heard his ten-year-old voice whisper, "This is what love is."

Hopson began finishing his grandparents' dance. He backpedaled, spun, cradled the broom gently then *big dip*. When he looked up, he was in front of the office door. It was wide open. Rome the janitor was standing there.

Orb glasses magnified Rome's eyes, making them as thick and shiny as maple syrup. He scratched his chin with a thumb permanently bent by arthritis. Then Rome peeped over the top of his glasses at Hopson. "Son, you need a woman."

Chapter Eleven

What a man needs in a woman and what a woman needs in a man can be different things at different times. But plans for the big payback put Imani and Hopson on the same path.

Right now she needed to get back at Taz, and Hopson needed to get back at Sherman. The two had finally talked and decided to meet the next day for lunch at a little diner two blocks off campus.

"I'm glad you called, Imani."

Imani took measure of Hopson's face, the strong features and the fine line of his smile. The eagerness of it. She readjusted her shoulder bag that happened to be light on cash and heavy on bills.

"I had to call. You seemed so serious." *And I'm through with Taz.* "I figured, hey, what do I have to lose?"

"Nothing at all." *And I have everything to gain by winning the bet.* "So tell me, how's your time? I mean, what exactly do you do for a living?"

"I'm a street musician. Then, you know, I'm a shampoo girl over at Shari's."

"Can you make it without being the shampoo girl?"

"I can cut back on the days, sure, if the money's right."

"What about street performing, Imani? I don't see any room for compromise there. That sidewalk show has to stop if you're working at the university."

"Excuse me? I can pull in twenty bucks a day doing that. *Tax-free.*"

"And you look common doing it."

"Says you. The people dropping dollars don't think so. They say I got it going on."

"And you do—next to the guys playing the plastic buckets with chopsticks."

"You wrong for that."

"Imani, I'm being honest. You're better than that."

"Meanin'?"

"Meaning, if you act, speak, and do common things, that's all you'll ever be and all you'll ever get out of life. Nothing more. If you act special, then you'll be special . . . and wonderful things will happen."

"How do you know?"

"I just do."

"C'mon, Hops. Don't play me. Sounds like you're making this up as you go along."

"Imani, everything I'm telling you is the truth."

"Is that right. So, like, what you got that's so special?"

"I can hit two notes on the scale and hear the beginning of four different songs. I can play my horn so long and so hard that the inside of my chest feels like it's on fire, and still I'd play until I burned up inside and would never be happier. Music that's right for you can make life phenomenal. That's what I have. That's what I want for you."

Imani felt a rush in her gut. She fought it. Imani fought it because she didn't want to admire this man too much. Admiration, she had found, made her vulnerable. She needed to be in control.

"So what do you think, Imani?"

"I think all this special jive is gonna cost you. A sister like me is looking to get paid, *not played.*" The words sounded cold, rather hoarse. Imani wanted to take them back, especially after she saw Hopson's wholesome gaze turn into a bruised stare.

"How much does a working girl get?" Hopson asked, his teeth barely parting.

"You make me sound cheap."

"We've already established what kind of woman you are. Now we're just negotiating the price."

Imani grabbed her glass of water and threw it in Hopson's face. She found glee in her own boldness and waited for his reaction.

Hopson blinked twice, then licked his lips. "How'd you know I was thirsty?"

A giggle broke loose in Imani's body. Then Hopson began to laugh a little as he grabbed a handful of napkins. "You know what, Imani?"

"What?"

"If we ever stop fighting each other and work together, we'll be dangerous."

"You ain't lying." Imani's laughter floated around their space like notes waiting to land in a song. She eased out of her side of the booth and squeezed in next to him and began helping him dry off. "There. That's a whole lot better."

Hopson grabbed Imani's hand and held it. Then he gently pushed her away. "We need to work together about three days out of the week. The music budget allowed funds for an assistant, which I never hired. Can you transcribe music?"

"Yeah, my father taught me. He used to be an arranger back in the day."

"Can you play any instruments?"

"Piano."

"Do you have a high school diploma?"

"Yeah."

"Then you're hired. The job pays one hundred and fifty dollars a week. How's that?"

Imani slid back into her seat. She held her hand out in a very businesslike fashion. "Deal."

Outside, Professor Sherman and Ahmad were walking down the street.

"Thanks again, Professor Sherman. I've been having trouble with my composition assignment for the last three days."

"No problem, Ahmad. You know I'm always there for you guys. Black folks have to reach back and help one another whenever they can."

"I'm glad somebody does. Professor Hopson acts like he doesn't want to be bothered half the time."

Sherman slowed down and glanced in the window of the diner. He saw Hopson with Imani.

"Speak of the devil. And he's eating a burger." Sherman turned to Ahmad and motioned with his head inside the diner. "There's Hopson now. Who's that girl? A transfer student?"

"No. She's a townie. I've seen her around the bus station, performing for tips."

Sherman paused, then began walking again with Ahmad. "Huh, that's weird. Real weird. I didn't think Mister High and Mighty would go for the around-the-way girls. Wonder what's going on there?"

"What's going on with my insurance check?" Maceo yelled into the phone.

He listened.

"I've been waiting for an inspector to come out to my place now for near about three weeks."

He listened.

"Nine-eleven? That was eons ago. Y'all still blaming everything on that. Bin Laden this. Bin Laden that. My name's Bin too . . . *been tired of waiting.*"

He listened again.

"I've got to start fixing up my place, lady. My daughter's staying with friends 'cause our upstairs apartment is too bad to live in. I can't have any performers in my club because that part of the building is wrecked. All I can do is open the bar. And that ain't drawing no crowd neither. I need that insurance money. Now it's due me. When y'all coming out?"

He listened some more.

"Now you talking like you got some sense. What day? Lady, 'as soon as we can' ain't no date. That's a hope. Who are you, Jesse Jackson? *Up with hope. Down with dope. Everybody wash with soap!* Hello? *Hell—oooohhhh?!*"

Maceo slammed down the telephone.

"No luck, Daddy?"

"Nope, but don't you worry about it, Imani. Your old man has got everything under control. Me and Taz'll think of something."

"Taz? I'm here. I'm bringing in money."

"And I 'preciate it too. I just don't wanna worry my baby any more than I have to."

"But I'm not a baby anymore, Daddy."

"But you'll always be my little girl."

"That's different from being treated like I'm not mature enough to handle stuff."

"Who does that?"

"You do. You confide in Taz more than you do me!"

"Speaking of Taz, have you talked to him yet?"

"Don't change the subject, Daddy."

"You changed it. Not me."

Imani turned and walked across the bar. They were in the front room. It was damaged the least by the fire, but there was still a smoky smell in the air.

"Oh that's real mature. Don't turn me no answer and walk away."

Imani continued to the piano and sat down.

Maceo came up behind her. "Hold on, now. You're not *that* grown. Girl, you better turn me an answer before I snatch your little butt off that bench."

"No." Imani sighed and began playing a slow, bluesy tune. "No, I have not talked to Taz."

"How come?"

"Don't know."

"Know what he's been doing?"

"Don't care."

"Taz has been in the studio working on some songs for you. Says he's got the music down tight."

"Well I've got a new job and I don't have time to be messing around with Taz."

"A job? What kind of a job?"

Imani smiled and she was surprised at the excitement in her own voice. "Over at the university as an assistant. I'm working in the music department."

"How'd that come about?"

"Well there's this professor named Hops."

"Who?"

"Hopson. I call him Hops. Anyway, he heard me rap and says I have talent and—"

"He made you an assistant? Filing and stuff?" Maceo huffed. He reached in his pocket and pulled out a package of cigarettes.

"Transcribing music," Imani said, irritated. She took the rumpled package out of her father's hand and crushed the last cigarette to bits.

Maceo took two steps back and pulled out a fresh package. "You ain't stopping no show, little lady. And you don't need to be taking no penny-ante university job when you could be in the studio with Taz making a CD."

"This professor thinks I have talent. He's gonna help me. I

plan on getting him to listen to some of my songs—the ones Taz can't find the time for."

Maceo raised his eyebrows. "Has this professor got connects in the music business?"

"Well, no."

"He promised to help promote your CD?"

"Well, no, he don't know about the CD."

"Well good goddamn, girl, where does the helping you part fall in at?" Maceo blew smoke in the air. "Huh?"

"After hours, we'll work in his office on music and—"

"Uh-huh. After hours. *Yeah right.* This professor is a man no doubt."

"So?"

"Good-looking?"

"Yeah."

"Imani, think, baby. This man is just trying to take advantage of you. You're young and you're pretty. What's a big-time college professor need with a downtown girl for an assistant when he's got a campus full of music majors right there, that's what I want to know."

Imani stood up, anger scorching her throat. "I'd look for Taz to say somethin' hateful like that. But not you, Daddy."

"Baby, you're setting yourself up for failure. That professor is not gonna try and help you, not really. That's not what he's after."

"Daddy, you act like I don't have talent."

"Shoot yeah, you got talent. You're my child."

"Okay then. Finally, you're giving me some credit."

"Imani, you're full of talent. And with Taz working with you there's no telling how far you'll go."

"Taz! Taz! Everybody in the neighborhood is always hollering about how talented Taz is. How big Taz is gonna be. What about me?"

"Every dynamite diva has a man arranging her work. Everybody knows that. Taz is that person for you. He's like family, and I don't have to worry about him doing you wrong."

"Naw, he won't do me wrong," Imani mumbled, "just get a lap dance with every wanna-be hoochie he meets."

"Now, baby. Throw that outcha mind. That's just a young stallion grazing the grass." Maceo laughed. "I've wrecked many a field in my day."

"*Ha-ha.* It's not funny to me, Daddy."

"Don't pout, baby. You know good and well that Taz cares for you. Y'all have a future together."

"This is not about together, Daddy. This is about me. Sometimes a woman has to do something just for her. Sometimes she has to see what she can get for herself. That's all I'm saying. This man is a big-time music professor. And he picked me to work with. At first I thought it was bull, 'cause you know how the university folks treat us."

Maceo held Imani in his arms. "That's all I'm saying. The 'haves' take advantage of the 'have-nots' whenever they can."

"But my gut tells me this is different, Daddy. On the real. I feel like it's gonna be different this time."

"I don't wanna see you hurt, baby. Imani, this music world can be so ugly. It can drag you down and crush you under its boot, the way I stomp on bugs in the cellar. At least I'm decent enough to clean up behind myself. The music industry will leave you squashed right there in public for all the world to see how you failed."

"Daddy, I want something new. I need something different than laying down Taz's tracks and performing in front of folks going Greyhound. I wanna feel something different. If not forever, just for now. I wanna see what it's like, being uptown."

"It might end up being a painful sight."

"*Whatever it is,* it's still a new view."

Maceo sat next to Imani on the piano. He began to play a song he wrote for his late wife. "Sure hate that your mama never got a chance to record this song. Needed lyrics. Sure is pretty."

"I wanna make her proud of me, Daddy."

"If she's peeping down from heaven she already is, baby."

Imani knew her mother's song by heart and hummed it now as she rested her head on her father's shoulder. She hummed the love song and dreamed of brighter horizons.

Chapter Twelve

Envy the sun that has horizons to brighten. Envy the bird that has wings to soar. Envy the lion that has the power to roar. But envy most the person who has the courage to seek change.

How much heart does it take to step into a situation where all your surroundings are different from anything else you've ever experienced?

Imani didn't know what to expect.

Neither did Professor Hopson.

The first morning they were a little stiff around each other. Almost shy, too polite. Too short with their answers, fidgeting in their seats. But the next day, things got better. Professor Hopson took Imani on a tour of the campus.

Arlington had been in Imani's backyard all along, and she never really paid any attention to it, except when she was a little girl sneaking onto the grounds to see the charity ball.

Each building was named for a great African-American. The science building was the George Washington Carver Center. The auditorium was the Paul Robeson Hall.

"Did you know that this campus was built entirely by ex-slaves?"

"No. I knew Frederick Douglass had something to do with starting it; learned that in grade school, but that's about all."

"He started a fund-raising drive in D.C. All the wealthy abolitionists gave. But the economy got bad, and the benefactors ran out of money."

"Then what?"

"Then he sent out a call to all the free black tradesmen. He wanted volunteers. See over there?"

Imani looked out over a field that was lined with trees.

"The tradesmen planted fresh vegetables. Raised some chickens. That's how they ate. They pitched tents. Slept in the mud. Worked in the hot sun. They lived off the land until they could finish this school. Arlington is one of the first black universities in this country."

Imani seemed a little bit embarrassed that she had grown up right here and didn't know more about the school. "I have to give Frederick Douglass and them some props. It was a good idea to have somewhere for folks like you to go."

"You mean, like *us.*"

"This place ain't for me, Hops. All you big ballers around here with a lot of money, this is your spot. I've had to hustle for everything I've got, and then some."

"And that's who this school is for, people who know how to work hard and who are smart. Didn't I just tell you about those ex-slaves? Did they have money? No. Fancy places to live? No."

"I'm talkin' about now, Hops. Today. There's a big nasty gap between the black folks that's got and those that don't."

"What's the gap?"

"Money. Clothes. Houses."

"All that's material stuff, Imani. Hit the lotto and you can have that. Street hustling will get it too. But the people here, the students, most are from poor and working-class families. Their pockets aren't fat but their potential is. Like yours. If you don't waste it, anything is possible."

"So what are you saying, Hops? Don't trip off the bling-bling cars and the fly crib?"

"Right."

"Just make the most out of what you have . . ."

"Inside . . ,"

". . . And all the rest will come?"

"Right. That's how we're going to turn you into a sophisticated jazz singer."

The two of them stopped walking. They were standing beneath a giant oak in the center of campus. Most of the students were already in class. From a window up above, Professor Sherman happened to glance out during one of his classes. *There's Professor Hopson and that girl again.* He watched them for a hot second before turning away from the window to finish his lecture.

Meanwhile Imani was content to let shade from the oak tree fall across her face as she wondered, *Is Hops for real? He talks a good game but does he have game?*

Hopson teased Imani. "I've got you thinking."

She smirked. "No you don't."

"Yes I do . . . yes, yes . . . ," and he poked her in the side.

She playfully slapped his hand away. "Quit it. Who knew you had a silly side?"

Professor Hopson grabbed the tree branch overhead with both hands. "I just want us to make the best out of this. I'll give it all I've got if you will. Okay?"

Maybe this won't be so bad after all, she thought. Then Imani answered, "Okay, black man."

"Imani, a black man is only gonna take so much shit off his woman." Taz was leaning on his car. It was the end of the day and he was waiting for Imani in front of Club Maceo. "You know that, right?"

Imani wanted to laugh; instead she walked right by him. Taz grabbed her arm. Imani bucked her eyes at him. He let her go.

"Do you want to talk to me, Taz?"

"What am I standing here for, my health?"

"One minute you're yellin'. The next minute you're acting like a little boy who's sorry. Which is it gonna be? You keep changing up."

"I'm changing up? Ain't you ah trip. You blew a little thing . . ."

"A *lap dance* that was going straight to booty-call status . . ."

". . . A *little thing* like showmanship all out of proportion. That's all the girl was doing. Giving a little showmanship."

"Are you sorry, Taz?"

"I ain't do nothing!"

"Please."

"That was her."

"See ya."

Taz grabbed Imani's arm again. Imani gritted her teeth. "Are you sorry?"

"Sorry that you're making something out of nothing, yeah."

Imani jerked her arm down. "Ever since we were kids you could never admit you were sorry about anything. What is that?"

Taz knew she was telling the truth. He didn't know where it came from. Maybe it was because he never seemed to be in a place long enough to feel totally comfortable that he could make mistakes, be wrong lest someone come and snatch him away, or worse, push him away. Taz knew she was telling the truth. She was rocking his boat. Shaking the brother up. *Don't let her know that. Be about business. Let that be the reason,* he thought.

"Imani, 'tween working at Shari's and this college job, I haven't seen you. We've got to work on my CD."

"Your CD?"

"Our CD. You know what I meant to say. Stop bugging, Imani. When can I get you in the studio?"

Imani was enjoying the fact that she had Taz angry and for once he was at her beck and call. "Don't know. I gotta work . . ."

"At the university." Taz finished her sentence. "All right.

Fuck it, then. You don't wanna be bothered. I don't wanna be bothered." Taz whipped out his cell phone and started dialing. "I'll just call one of my boys and go hang."

Imani spun around. She stomped inside the club and slammed the door.

Taz got no answer. Then and only then did he realize that he truly wanted to talk to a friend. Frustrated, he mumbled, "Biggie. Where you at player?"

Biggie was between a rock and a .357 Magnum.

"What's with the gun?" Biggie asked.

The mailman was shaking. "I don't have the money."

The two men were on a run-down side street in the down-town neighborhood. There was one high-rise project on the corner. That was all. The rest of the street was vacant lots and abandoned buildings.

"Did you grow up around here?" Biggie asked, never looking at the gun, always looking at the man. "Huh?"

The mailman shook his head.

"Thought not. 'Cause if you did, you'd know that if you pull a gun, you shoot. It's not a door or a coat. You don't hold it."

The mailman was sweating.

"Put it down or shoot."

"I'm scared."

Biggie shrugged. "Think about what you're doing."

The body reacts before the mind. Sweat began pulsing out of the mailman's brow. His chest pumped salty water too. He was practically leaking.

Biggie whipped his hand up and knocked the gun out of the mailman's hand. Next he gut-punched him twice with a left, then a right. The mailman hit his knees and fell over on his side. Then Biggie kicked him. *And kicked him. And kicked him.*

Later Mr. Watson would say, "Shame about what happened to the mailman."

Biggie hadn't said a word. Claude just grinned.

"The folks up in the projects saw him pull a piece on you, Biggie. Told me all about it." Mr. Watson pulled an expensive cigar out of his pocket. "Some of those same folks owe me money." He lit the cigar. "They might try to pull something similar."

"And wind up in intensive care like him?" Biggie balked. "I don't think so."

Mr. Watson blew smoke rings. Then looked at the cigar. "Still. We can't be too careful. For the next few weeks, if you go up around that project, anywhere around there, I want you boys to collect together. You and Claude."

The two enforcers looked at each other cross-eyed.

"You boys do like I say. And that's it."

Chapter Thirteen

While Mr. Watson was being cautious, Professor Hopson decided to take a chance on a plan. He hoped it would help him get through to Imani.

He told her to start bringing in magazines and he would too; they would talk about the stories to get a feel for how the other thought and reacted to things. It would be an icebreaker of sorts.

That was part one; part two would shake Imani up.

Imani brought in *Vibe*. Hopson brought in *Newsweek*.

The next day he pulled out a tape recorder. "I recorded our conversation yesterday."

"What?" she said in surprise. "Who are you? The FBI or something?"

"Don't get mad. I just wanted to make a point. Listen to how you sound. Remember when we were talking about that *Vibe* article on the rapper accused of sexual assault?"

Imani nodded and Hopson played the tape: *"Hops, they need to put that mo-fo up under the jail. He's a rapper and I'm a rapper but hey, what they did to that girl up in that hotel room was foul. She didn't have that comin'. That makes me mad. Lock his ass up."*

"Then we talked about the Republican tax plan in *Newsweek.* Remember, Imani?"

"Their track record is screwed up. They don't think about the little man. The regular working guy, hustlin' to make a living like my daddy. Remember the trickle-down theory? What was that about? Tricklin' down is like peein'. It stinks. We need more money for schools, housing for the homeless. And that's real. I'm with the Democrats on that. We gotta get some goodies for the people."

Imani's voice sounded raw, harsh. She blushed. "Is that me?"

Hopson nodded.

Imani didn't say anything.

"If I told you you use too much slang and sound too hard, you would say that I was picking on you. But I'm not. It's constructive criticism. That's why I recorded you. To play it back and let you hear it for yourself."

Imani shrugged. "That's just me."

"I'm not asking you to totally change. But the cursing and slang is unbecoming. I want you to be a jazz diva. You're pretty. Talented. And when people talk to you after you perform, or interview you, you don't want to sound like a 'hood rat."

Imani felt a rush of heat around her ears. She sat up in the office chair. "So you think you can just change me for a hundred and fifty dollars a week?"

"I'm not asking you to change how you think, change your political party. I'm just saying that how you present ideas and opinions reflects on you. How you communicate is important, Imani. Being hard plays well onstage in the rap world but not for jazz. You have style. I'm just trying to bring it out, that's all."

Hopson left the tape recorder on the desk.

Imani picked it up, rewound the tape, and played it. She quickly cut it off after a couple of words. Imani thought a moment, holding it against her chin.

The next day they began grammar lessons. Breath-control

lessons. Imani would sit in a chair, balancing a notebook on her head while facing a long, lit candle at the end of the desk. Hopson sat on the edge of the desk.

"A-E-I-O-U." Imani would direct her voice forward, and if the flame flickered or blew out, she was too breathy and popping her syllables. They did this off and on, listening to some jazz divas in between. Hopson pointed out their crisp, clean sound, every syllable of a word hit hard like a high note.

That evening Imani went to work at the salon.

"Look what the wind blew in," Ma June teased with a smile. Before Imani could close the door behind her, the scrawny neighborhood thief slipped through the door with two shopping bags from an elite uptown store.

"Not you, mister!" Ma June scolded him. "No crackheads in here trying to sell us junk.

"I beg your pardon." He sucked air. "I'll have you know I'm a reefer-head."

"Only half as bad, but still bad enough." Ma June tried to push him back out the door. "Good-bye."

"But I got Pradas!" he yelled, holding up the bags.

"I *know* you got *problems.* We all got problems. See ya." Ma June slammed the door in his face. "How's the new job going, baby?"

"Fine."

"You don't sound fine. Anything new will be hard at first. Just relax." Ma June kissed her on the cheek. "Shari's in the basement counting stock."

Imani went downstairs.

"You know I must love you, girl." Shari had a clipboard in her hand checking off boxes. "I'm down here counting my own stock."

"Hand it here."

Shari gave Imani the clipboard and started back upstairs. She stopped and watched her friend for a minute. Shari came right back down, looked at the clipboard, then took it out of Imani's hand. She grabbed Imani by the shoulders and sat her down on a stool in the corner.

"Now . . . what's wrong?"

"Nothing, Shari."

"Please. You're checking off 'perm' for 'conditioner' and you got me ordering a case of platinum dye instead of basic black. Every woman up in here will be either bald-headed like Michael Jordan or white-headed like Halle Berry in *X-Men*. Where's your mind?"

"I'm cool."

"How's the university thing going?"

"It's a little strange. We haven't done any music yet, not really. We've been talking, and he told me to stop using so much slang. Watch my grammar and all that."

"What's that got to do with singing?"

"It's the jazz style and everything." Imani shrugged. "It's more technical. It's more work than I thought."

"You sound kindah stressed. I thought you did this to get back at Taz and make a little money at the same time?"

"That's the plan."

"You're not getting interested in the man, are you?" Shari asked. "You gotta watch those uptown guys."

"No, it's not that."

"What then? I mean, I know you're mad at Taz and wanna shake his cheating butt up. But you got this funny look on your face. I don't like it. Something's up."

"I kindah . . . wanna see . . . maybe . . . how I'd be as a jazz singer. Would it be so bad?"

"But you love rap. You own the stage when you rap, Imani."

"I know, Shari. But you know my mama was a jazz singer. Before? I didn't wanna follow in her footsteps. Maybe I was afraid. But now? Hey, I kindah want to see how it would be to chase her dream."

"Imani, changing yourself is a dangerous game, girl. Don't fool around and hurt yourself trying to be something you're not."

"I just wanna try new things. What's wrong with that? The old never changes and it don't move. It'll always be there to fall back on. I'm just a little rattled 'cause everything is so new to me, Shari. That's all."

"Okay, tell that corny-ass professor he better not hurt my girl. I don't wanna have to jack him up."

"Don't worry about him, Shari. I've got something up my sleeve. Hops is always trying to show me something, I'm going to show him a *little something-something.*"

After about an hour, Imani grumped. "Enough, please."

"You can go a little while longer. It won't kill you."

"I get it. I'm cutting back on the slang. We've been doing this for a couple of weeks now. It's just a matter of time, let's move on to the music, Hops."

"This is first. I want you to enunciate. In jazz you have to hit your notes *and* your words on point. Proper diction. Crisp enunciation."

"Now I know why you're so corny, Hops."

"And why is that?"

"Because you ain't got—"

"Don't have."

"That too. No soul."

"You heard me play the horn? How could you say that?"

Imani pulled out the tape recorder that he had used on her. "Payback is a dog as we say in the 'hood, baby."

"Slang."

"I called time-out."

"C'mon, Imani. There are no time-outs."

She hit the play button on the recorder: "Your goal is to enunciate each syllable. The timbre of the note should be precise.

Breath control is essential. Focus and concentrate on your sound and the emotion you hope to convey."

Hopson looked mad that Imani had taped him from earlier.

"Don't get mad. Turnabout is fair play."

Hopson smirked a little.

"Admit it, Hops. Don't you sound like a stuffy old man? A stuffy old man with no soul?"

"If that's true—and mind you, Imani, I'm not saying that it is—how would you go about getting me some?"

"I'd be the teacher and you'd be the student then. How's that for flipping the script? I'd be showing you something new."

"Oh really?"

"Yes really. Somewhere where there's no uptown *or* downtown. Everybody's equal."

The place where everybody is equal is the house of God. The little church that Imani took Hopson to was only a mile away from the university. It was a plain, white-frame structure with a triangular roof, nestled behind a highway entrance ramp. It made the church look like a hanky sticking out of a deacon's breast pocket.

The wide-brim hats on the elders' row were as varied and brilliant in color as the sections of a rainbow. Cardboard hand fans flitted in the air like hovering moths; slight was the breeze, whimsical was the sight.

They were running a little late and church had already started. Hopson had tried to beg out of it, claiming he had some research to do. Imani had to threaten Hopson with *both* a work stoppage *and* a butt kicking in order to get him to come.

They were waiting to be let into the sanctuary after the morning prayer was said. The senior ushers in their white starched uniforms greeted Imani with a series of "Hey baby"s. She had on a Sunday church dress, well-tailored but not tight-fitting, in a perky shade of blue. Small diamond earrings. A watch. Three-inch heels. Stockings.

"Did I tell you how pretty you look today?" Professor Hopson said as they waited for the doors to open so they could be seated.

"Yeah. Thanks."

"You look like a lady. When you come to work, in all those big hip-hop jerseys or super-tight jeans and the big eighteen-wheeler earrings, it's too masculine, or too gangster for someone as pretty as you. Dress pretty. Dress more like a lady."

Normally what he said might have made Imani mad. Like he was trying to hate. Signify. But Imani knew him much better by now. He was genuinely trying to be real, helpful, and giving. Weren't they in the house of the Lord? So she gave back.

"Okay. I'll try if you try."

"What do you mean?"

"I mean you need to update your look. A little changing on your part wouldn't hurt either, Hops."

He started fidgeting with his clothes.

Imani stepped back and checked the brother out. "That suit is waaaaay too old for you. The cut. And why not wear some slacks and a nice shirt? No suit at all. And look at your shoes, man. My daddy has shoes like that and, yes they are classics, but throw some polish on the bad boys, would ya?"

Normally Hopson would be offended. But he looked into Imani's eyes and saw that she was speaking from the heart. Besides, he had heard it before. Only from Professor Sherman. Maybe he *could* get some new clothes, nothing *too* out there, but still a little more up-to-date. "Okay, Imani. I'll try too."

The ushers swung the glass doors open and welcomed them forward, waving in their crisp white gloves.

"Hey, Hops. You said you were Catholic, right?"

"Right."

Imani and Hopson began walking forward. "Then I should warn you. This is a sanctified church."

"Meaning what?"

Imani shoved Hopson to the left as a petite little man jumped into the aisle and started doing a dance that looked like an Indian parading around a campfire. *"Thank you Jesus! He's good, so good!"*

"Meaning *that.*"

Professor Hopson's eyes got wide as he took in all the movement. People were rocking back and forth, some sitting and some standing. Others were shouting fearlessly. The organist was pounding the keys.

Imani headed for her regular row. There was space for two in the middle. Hopson asked the people on the end, "Would you slide down?"

The elderly couple on the end stopped in midshout. "We've been sitting here every Sunday for the past thirty years. You slide, son."

Imani laughed.

Hopson and Imani squeezed by and made it to the middle of the row. Two heavyset saints sat on either side of them.

"Hops, one thing you have to remember sitting here."

"What's that?"

"See the sister next to you?"

Hopson went to turn his head.

"Don't look. See the one next to me?"

Hopson went to lean up.

"Don't look. Just glance at them out of the corner of your eye. Now if they start moaning? Slide to the left. If they jump up, then duck down."

"What?"

A little boy was turned around in the pew in front of them. He had on a dark blue suit, a white shirt, and bow tie. He grinned a bucktoothed smile. "She said slide and duck."

"Slide and duck?"

The preacher was an older man, spotty gray temples, high white collar, stomach pouched out from countless homemade sweets eaten while visiting the sick and shut-in.

His voice boomed in the small church, radiating confidence, radiating direction. He spoke to the masses but seemed to be having an intimate chat with each individual.

"Will you be *right* and *ready* when Jesus calls? Will you, saints?"

The heavyset saint sitting next to Hopson closed her eyes and started humming, sweat creeping down her brow. Some of the curls of saltwater got trapped in the folds of her neck. She hummed louder.

Hopson slid left. Imani nudged him right. "That was a hum, not a moan."

"What's the difference?"

Imani and the little boy both said, "You'll see."

The preacher's chest began to heave as his voice escalated and pushed up the hopes of those sitting in front of him. Intense eyes locked in on him, following his every hand wave and neck swivel.

"Stop lying. Stop cheating. Stop backsliding . . ."

The litany of what to stop was ongoing until the floor started to creak from folks stomping their feet. The cardboard fans went into overdrive.

"*Stop-stop-stop-stop* . . ." The preacher sounded like a machine gun firing.

The heavyset saint next to Hopson started to moan. But everyone else was so loud, he barely heard her. Then the moan got really *loud.* Hopson ducked. All of a sudden she rammed her hips to the right . . . Hopson slid forward on the slick wooden pew and bumped his lowered head on the hymnal rack.

"Ouch!"

Just as he started to rise, the woman started rocking. As soon as his head was up, she jumped up and flung her arms out, fists balled up in knots. "Help me, Lord!"

She cracked him right across the face. He slumped down on one knee.

The little boy laughed, pointing down. "You ducked when you was supposed to slide, and you slid when you was supposed to duck."

The woman was rocking and rolling now. Hopson tried to get up but ducked down as the heavy arms flayed the air.

"Stay down!" the little boy advised.

Imani was holding his shoulders.

"Sinners! Sinners!" She flayed the air. "Sinners!"

Suddenly a set of deacons came over to carry the woman out. The first man came in alone. She swung her arm and knocked his glasses off. They spun into orbit and hit the top of the pew, breaking. Then she took him out with a spinning hip check.

"Stay down," Imani said, now hunched behind Hopson.

The other deacons waiting to go in started taking off their glasses, their suit jackets . . . one man even took and popped his dentures out into a white hanky. *Teeth are expensive.* "I'll help," Hopson said over his shoulder to Imani.

"Bad move," she said trying to pull his coat. But Hopson eased up and grabbed the woman's arm. She wrapped the other one around his neck and started jumping up and down. *"Save me. Save. Save me."*

"Somebody save *me!*" Hopson moaned as he began to lose air as the billowy arms locked tighter and tighter around him.

Finally the deacon army rushed in and grabbed the woman every which a'way. When she finally did let Hopson loose, he slumped onto the pew, his eyes practically crossed.

Someone asked, "Did the Holy Spirit get him?"

"No," Imani said, fanning Hopson with a cardboard picture of Dr. King. "Sister Boyd."

The choir was now up and singing. Their voices were full, ringing up against the rafters, floating down and rocking the congregation's worries away.

Their soulful singing and the cool air from the fan soothed Hopson. He opened his eyes.

"You okay?" Imani asked.

"Yeah," Hopson said. "The choir is great."

She just hugged him.

Chapter Fourteen

It's easy to hug someone else. But one of the hardest things in the world for us to do is to hug ourselves. How can you know exactly what you need to do to *feel* the best that you can, and at the same time *do* the best that you can with what you have in your soul?

It's such a tripped-out adventure with zigs and zags plus the ups and downs. It makes you crazy sometimes. Makes your heart flutter sometimes. Or like the old rap song says, makes you wonder how you keep from going under.

But when you find a path that you have the courage to travel, every experience becomes a boost for your confidence. And if you have someone to share that with, you both will grow.

"You're struggling, Imani."

Professor Hopson had given her some sheet music from a traditional jazz piece. It had tricky riffs and changes in key, and he wanted her to practice exerting power on finesse vocals. He leaned over and touched her shoulder.

"Are you having trouble reading the music?"

"No."

"But you're not hitting the notes. Can't you hear it? The sound I want is very retro. That's what I'm trying to get out of you."

"I'm trying, Hops."

"I know." He took note of her slumped shoulders. Her eyelids looked heavy. Imani hadn't been getting much sleep with working at Shari's and the university too. "C'mon, Imani. We're going on a field trip."

Imani had just enough energy to laugh. "Last field trip I took was in the third grade."

"Where to?"

"The zoo. Got my first tongue kiss, right behind the lion's den. Smacked the taste out of Taz's mouth too."

"Well don't beat me up if you don't like where we're going. Just c'mon."

"Where?"

"Trust me."

They got in Hopson's car and hit the highway. Imani liked surprises and spontaneous whims. She felt relaxed. Her long braids were streaming behind her like silk ribbons in the wind. Imani nestled her body low into the passenger side of the two-seater BMW.

In the wind, she seemed to hear a voice ask what she was hoping for, and the answer she returned, with a nervous batting of the eyes, quick anxious breaths, sort of Morse-code emotion, was an answer that only the best seemed possible.

Professor Hopson took Imani twenty miles away to a small town that had a little row of shops as soon as you exited the highway. They parked at the end of the block and walked to a huge storefront. It had a picture window plastered with old album covers from Styx, Parliament, Ella Fitzgerald, Louie Armstrong.

"How'd you find this place?" Imani cupped her hands against the window and peeped in. "It's mad chaos up in there. *But I likes. I likes.*"

Hopson winked at her.

Inside the shop owner could barely be seen behind a stack of cardboard album covers. All you saw were gnarled hands with turtle-shell knuckles quickly slipping black disks in and out of their jackets. Cotton balls soaked in alcohol were strewn about the counter like scattered rain clouds in the sky.

The shop owner picked up a piece of cotton and gently stroked circles along the crusty grooves of the old albums.

"Joe," Hopson said, stepping up to the counter with Imani.

He stuck his head out. Feathers of blond hair barely covered his freckled bald dome. Round glasses slid halfway down his nose. He wore a white shirt, no collar, and a vest with a pocket that was stuffed with chewed-on pencils. "Professor, how are you?"

"Good. Brought a friend. This is Imani."

"Hi."

"Pretty," Joe said, still massaging the vinyl records.

Hopson glanced at her. "Yes she is." And he felt a sense of pride. "I'll give her the grand tour."

The place was packed with records: albums by one-hit wonders and collectibles by the famous. Some were in order. Others were stuck in piles labeled Miscellaneous. Some were on the floor, crammed in boxes, without their covers, comfortable in this old folks' home for the hot-wax sounds of great musicians from the last millennium.

Hopson had discovered the place by accident and fallen in love with it by fate. Without thinking he grabbed Imani's hand. Professor Hopson felt so much joy in sharing the place with her because he knew Imani loved music and would appreciate it.

"Imani, see this old booth?"

"Yeah, like who needs a phone booth now that everybody's got a cell?"

"It's not a telephone."

"What is it then, Hops?"

"A listening booth. This is how it was done in the old days. You go inside, shut the glass door, and then play your record first, to make sure you wanna buy it."

"Sweet."

"There's already something good on the turntable too."

Hopson put the record on. It played.

"Makes you appreciate CDs, Hops. None of that hissing and popping."

"But listen to her technique. This is Gwen Highman. She was huge in the thirties. But now? People have forgotten all about her."

The ghostly sound of the jazz singer wrapped the two young folks in a rhythmic blanket, nestling them together in one mind, one spirit. Imani found an old Ella Fitzgerald album and put on a cut she had heard her father play.

So they took turns, picking songs they knew and then taking a shot in the dark, trying cuts they'd never heard. They critiqued the person's style, the arrangement, and the musicianship. They laughed out loud at a couple of old comedy albums and the corny jokes, the fake laugh tracks. And together in the small space they grew closer. The short time of knowing someone can expand in a common passion, a common goal, and become a catalyst.

In the dusty record den, a spark began as they laughed and shared music, singing along on songs they knew. Hopson tapped out beats on the wooden counter inside the listening booth. Imani threw out some rhymes to the music of a couple of instrumental jazz albums.

When it was time to go, Imani stopped to talk to the shop owner, Joe. "I just wanna tell him how much I love his store. I'll be right out."

"Okay. I'll get the car."

Imani waited until he left. "Hey Joe, can you look for an album for me? It's called *Songs from the Heart.*"

Joe put pencil to pad and began scribbling down the info.

"If you find it, could you call me? I'll give you my cell phone number. It's very important. I don't care how much it costs. If you find it, get it."

"Will do."

Imani's eyes lit up. They glowed with the possibility that a copy of her mother's album might be found.

But Imani wasn't the only person searching. Professor Sherman was searching for answers. He wanted to know why Professor Hopson was helping Imani.

It was a week later. Professor Sherman and a couple of music students were walking across the yard together. They were on the backside of Robeson Hall. Rome the janitor had the rear doors open. He was tossing out some old furniture.

A lovely voice flowed through the door, hanging in the air. It was in bits and pieces, sparkling and bright, occasionally fading like a star flickers in the sky.

The sound brought Professor Sherman and the students to a dead stop. They looked and couldn't see anyone. They moved forward, drawn by the voice. It was the sound of pure talent trying to grow. It was as if a newborn was pecking through a shell, struggling to get out.

They stepped past Rome. Sherman asked him, "Who is that singing?"

He scratched his head. "Somebody Professor Hopson knows. Nice girl."

"She's got talent," one of the students said.

"Needs work," Professor Sherman added as he headed deeper inside. "I'll see you guys later. Don't be late for class."

He walked inside alone, stopping at the last row of seats, hidden by the sun that cast a veil of yellow against his back. Up ahead onstage was Professor Hopson at the piano and Imani by his side.

She looked hesitant. Cutting her eyes at him every now and then to be reassured. He was nodding. Shaking his head. Pointing up for a higher register.

But her voice, even in this infant stage of confidence, was

rich and pure. It made you feel warm inside. Made you want to hear more. Professor Sherman listened for as long as he could before going to class himself. But the picture of Imani and Hopson together stayed with him long afterwards. *Can you imagine it? Hopson training someone. Hopson taking a passionate one-on-one-interest in someone.*

This was something new.

It was as new as the around-the-way girl now on campus. Who was she? What was she doing at Arlington? Why was Hopson helping her? Inquiring minds wanted to know. So one morning Professor Sherman decided to ask.

"What's going on with you and that girl?" Sherman handed Hopson a cup of herbal tea from Starbucks.

"What girl?" Hopson said, taking a sip of tea.

"Negro, please." Sherman took a gulp of coffee. "The one coming and going in and out of your office. Heard her singing in Robeson Hall too. What's her name?"

"You mean Imani?"

"Yeah," Sherman helped sarcastically. "That pretty around-the-way girl. Not a student."

"Oh her. *That girl.*"

"Quit it, man. What's the deal?"

Professor Hopson shrugged. "Nothing much. She's working for me. That's all. I needed an assistant."

"You needed help? You?"

"Transcribing music and stuff."

"Professor Control Freak? I can't believe you *thought* you needed help. Besides, since when did the music department have enough money for an extra assistant? The budget is shot to hell as it is."

"Don't say anything to her or anybody else, Sherman. I'm coming out of pocket myself."

Professor Sherman walked around the office desk, glancing at the papers, finishing up his coffee.

Hopson loved the fact that Sherman didn't have a clue. "Don't you have something to do? Something besides bugging me?"

"No. This is too good. Its kindah funny."

"Funny how?"

"Well, I notice you're sporting some new suits. Still too conservative for my taste but it's kindah cool for you. I'm *sure* that's her influence."

Professor Hopson just rolled his eyes.

"Add that to the fact that you're paying this woman out of pocket. I mean, think about it. You *never* spend any extra time with the music students. So what's so special about this girl?"

"She's from the low end of town and needed a job. She's got some musical talent too. Told her I'd give a listen every once in a while. Show her a few things." Hopson still didn't reveal the bet he had with Chairman Perkins. "She's pretty raw."

"When did you get to be so helpful?" Professor Sherman sat on the edge of the desk.

"You act like I'm some kind of monster or something. I work very hard and when I see talent, I want to draw it out."

"Usually you're so wrapped up in your own research, compositions, and goals that you don't have time for anyone else. I thought you had something else in mind. You know, like, grooming yourself for one of those big-time universities?"

"Maybe. Maybe not." Professor Hopson didn't want Sherman to know that he *really had been* testing the academic waters. "But I'll say this. I'll bet their department chairs don't ride the faculty like Perkins does."

"He just wants the best out of us. That's all. He's a race man like me. He'll die on a black college campus. But you, who knows?"

"Don't try to judge me, Sherman."

"I'm not. You work hard, man. You love music too. I'm not judging you but I sure can't figure you out. I just don't see you helping this uh-huh . . ."

"Imani."

"Right, Imani. It's just not like you to tear yourself away from your own work. Not unless there's more to it."

"Well there's not." Professor Hopson drained the rest of his tea and shot the cup at the wastepaper basket.

He missed.

Professor Sherman killed the rest of his coffee and shot the cup at the wastepaper basket.

Nothing but net.

Chapter Fifteen

Professor Sherman wasn't the only one *dead on target.*

Imani was determined to flip the script, to show Hopson the songwriting talent she had. But like Taz, he was heavy-handed, wanted to run things, have everything his own way when it came to music.

"Imani . . . we gotta work harder on my arrangements. You're making progress. But I don't want good. I want great."

"I want great," Imani challenged, "but I want to have a say too. You remind me of Taz sometimes, you know that?"

Professor Hopson didn't take the remark lightly. He saw defiance. He felt her challenging him. He felt her fighting him. Imani didn't say it, but when she crossed her arms he *knew* she wasn't about to sing another note for him.

I'm giving you space, Imani thought. *Man, I'm giving you an opportunity to show that you can share, that you respect my mind and not just my voice. C'mon, Hops. C'mon.*

Professor Hopson sighed heavily, then glanced down at Imani's feet. He saw her notebook. He picked it up and handed it to her.

"Okay. Show me something."

A pleased smile etched its way across Imani's face. She

rocked back in the chair, then stood up, closed her eyes, and busted off one of her own rhymes, one that Taz would never like because it wasn't hard enough. One Hopson would never really like because it wasn't sophisticated enough. One she loved the hell out of because it was real.

"A-E-I . . . I is for Imani, a queen in her own right . . ." The words filled the zigzagging cracks of the two musical worlds that were at war inside of her. Imani closed her eyes and the words flowed from her insides the way the source of a river bubbles up and overflows the surrounding banks.

Imani spoke of the heartache that often rocks a black girl's heart, a heart left feeling lonesome after being shown the cold shoulder by the world. A heart left uncuddled, accustomed to the hits and misses of love. These things that Imani had felt, these things that she had seen, were wrapped in her rhymes, not pretty and presentable in ribbons but bandaged and in a fit of healing.

Imani's brain swelled with thoughts. Some internal power pushed the words up from her gut so fast and so hard that her tongue lashed against the back of her teeth the way loose curtains whip against open windows during a storm.

Hopson was struck still. Her voice had a beautiful timbre. He marveled at the way the curve of her mouth formed the shape of an unfinished kiss after each syllable.

When Imani finished, she opened her eyes and waited for him to respond.

"Imani, if you can stop me cold with mere words, then imagine what you can do to the world singing a full-bodied song? Didn't I tell you you were special?"

Imani expected criticism and got praise. She was speechless. Imani was so taken aback that she plopped back down in the chair and just grinned.

Hopson was pleasantly paused too. He admired the raw talent of this woman. But he had to get her to nail the arrangements he planned for the ball. He couldn't possibly slip in any rap, no matter how good it was. He said easily, "Can we try the jazz ballad again?"

Imani felt like a dissed wordsmith.

Suddenly the door opened. "Professor Hopson?"

It was Chairman Perkins. "I thought I heard voices when I was walking by."

"Oh," Imani said, recognizing the man who had saved her from the security guard more than a month ago. "That was me you heard. I was rapping. I met you on the yard, remember?"

"Yes." Chairman Perkins smiled at Imani. He frowned at Hopson. "Professor, a moment alone, please?"

"Well look y'all"—Imani corrected herself—"I mean, you two gentlemen obviously need to talk."

"Same time tomorrow, Imani?"

"Sure." She didn't want to show her disappointment over Hopson not wanting to include her rhyme. So Imani turned and got busy gathering her jacket, tapes, and her notebook.

"Don't forget, Imani. Make sure you listen to those jazz tapes I gave you."

Hopson watched her leave. Chairman Perkins's eyes flashed with anger. "You have less than two months to get her ready if you're going to have *any chance* at all of proving your point and winning our bet."

"I know the ball is in less than two months. I know."

Did either man notice? *The door didn't close all the way.* A shadowy figure walked up and stopped to eavesdrop.

"I've been putting Professor Sherman on hold about whose paper I will submit to the grant contest because I *thought* you were seriously trying to work."

"But we are."

"Did I hear her singing something by Ella?"

"Well no, but—"

"I heard rap ringing down the hallway. I'm a man of limited

patience. You need to show me that you're serious or I'll stop this charade right now—bet or no bet—and just submit Professor Sherman's paper and be done with it. You'll lose."

"Don't do that—she can—she *will* prove my theory."

"I'm ready to call this whole thing quits."

"You don't have to believe in us, Chairman. But I do. I know I can turn Imani into a sophisticated jazz singer."

"Well," Chairman Perkins relented, "light a fire under her butt, Hopson, or it's going to cost you dearly."

What price will we pay for love? Do we marvel at it like a precious item in the store window, saving up until we can finally have it wrapped and handed to us? Then do we hold it dear?

If someone gives it to us, wrapped pretty, as a gift, does it have the same value as when we viewed it from afar and had to work so hard to get it?

Imani handed her love to Taz gift-wrapped, free of charge when they were stepping onto puberty's stage. He accepted it like it was his birthright. Since then Taz had never really done anything to pay for it.

It was the first love offering Taz had ever received. So young and so battered emotionally by parental rejection, he was almost afraid to accept it. *Imani had chased him. Gone after him. Done things for him.* She shared her lunch money with Taz when his pockets were empty. She told him he was talented and she oughtah know, because music was in her blood.

After Taz accepted the love offering and they entered their teenage years, there was a change. Then Taz became afraid that he would lose it; that's when he became super possessive, smothering even, trying to hold it so close that the joy was almost squeezed out of it. Anytime another boy looked at Imani, Taz wanted to fight him or get Biggie to fight the kid for him.

When true manhood arrived, Taz grew cocky and once again

took Imani's love offering for granted. Why work at keeping it? Where was she going? Nowhere, he thought. I got the girl's heart on lockdown.

And what we think we cannot lose, we don't bother to protect.

"Imani, you must be crazy playing me off like this."

Taz was standing in the doorway of the little storage area that Shari had converted into a temporary bedroom for her friend.

"How'd you get in here? Nobody's home but me. Shari and Baby are spending the night at her mama's house."

"Biggie let me in. Shari gave him a key."

Imani's heart raced at the sight of her shunned lover. She hadn't been this close to him in a long time. "Biggie," she called out as Taz moved slowly towards her, "Shari's not going to like you letting people in when she's not here."

"Biggie's long gone, girl." Taz was now two steps away from Imani. "He had some business. We're alone."

Taz's confidence was slick and enticing. He stalked within her space the way lions patrol their jungles. He seemed determined yet coy. Taz circled Imani. She stood still wondering what he would do, what he would say.

"Did you miss me?" Taz asked.

Imani didn't answer but knew that she had. Hated that she still did. And she wanted so bad to trip Taz up and expose him for the scrub he had been that she gritted her teeth.

But something stopped her voice from serving up her hurt. Was it because she wasn't sure that it would be enough to snap some sense into this man? Or was it because her love for Taz was too thick in her throat, two heavy to go down and too sweet to throw up.

"Yes, yes, Imani. I can feel you, girl. That's what's up. I can feel you like my own toes wiggling inside my shoes."

Imani didn't move.

Taz placed his hands on her arms and barely held her as if the slightest friction would make her crack and fall to the floor in a gazillion pieces.

"It's hot in here, baby."

Next Taz blew a cool stream of air across her neck, trying to make a wish . . . a wish that would be them, undressed, wrapped up in each other's skin, passionately sinking deeper and deeper.

"Is it hot, Imani?"

"It's getting there," Imani said softly, biting her bottom lip. She glanced at Taz and instead of seeing the man who had angered and hurt her, she saw the little boy who stayed in a house with no parents and no love who always seemed to need affection.

Taz ran the tip of his tongue along the rim of her ear.

Imani's head dropped back as warmth began brewing in the pit of her stomach.

"Do you want it up against the wall?"

Imani heard Hopson's voice: *Don't be common.*

"Do you want it on the floor?"

Be a lady, Imani.

"Do you want it in that rocking chair?"

Imani recalled a story she'd read in one of the books Hopson had given her. "I want you to love me like I'm a queen and it's your duty to protect my love and my honor."

She went there on a brother.

"This is something new and kinky, ain't it?"

He went there on a sister.

So Imani showed him how she didn't want to be rushed and how she didn't want to be pawed. That frantic wasn't passion, just hurry. Petals on a drooping flower. She showed him how a sweet, lingering kiss can be more pleasing than skin-bruising neck sucking. She showed him how a soft, body-length caress can be more pleasing than machine-inspired strokes. She showed him how a man should love a lady.

"How was that, baby?" Taz asked as they lay holding each other afterwards. "I feel waxed but it was so different from our regular skins. How'd it do you?"

"It was sweet. I feel pleased and satisfied."

"You're talking kindah funny, girl. That's that college talk. I know you've been hiding out in some job over there at the university. I like it in you, Imani. You're doing everything you can to help your daddy get his finances together, but truth is we've gotta get back to the studio and finish our CD. You need to squash that university job."

"You work, why can't I?"

"I load mail trucks because I gotta pay bills, Imani. Not because I like it. Why waste time at that dry university all day? You were doing cool with the street show. Plus that kept you sharp."

"I'm learning new things. Hops is so different—"

"Who's Hops?"

"Professor Hopson. He's got a PhD. The man's a musical genius; he's been written up in a bunch of journals. Let me show you one." Imani did but Taz wasn't impressed.

"Piss on paper praise. My man got any Grammys?"

"No."

"Then later for him. You need to get back in the studio with me. Please, baby, do it for the Taz man? Huh?" He began to cuddle and smooch Imani. She enjoyed it for a moment, then squirmed away. "Where you going?"

"Just to get some water. Would you like some?"

"Hey, I kindah like these manners that Hops guy is teaching you. Before, you'd tell me to get up and get my own."

"Manners wouldn't hurt you either. *Do you want some water or not?*"

"Yes, please, thank you."

Taz pulled the covers up as Imani headed for the kitchen. His cell phone rang. Taz found his pants and answered it. Biggie was on the other end.

Imani put ice cubes in the glasses, poured the drinks, and set them on a tray. *Maybe I can go back in the studio,* she thought. *Taz has been working pretty hard. Hops wouldn't like that though,* she reasoned. *But maybe if I just went to finish the CD, it wouldn't mess up what we're trying to do at the university.*

"Yeah, Biggie man, I hit that. And just like we said, that's all she needed . . ."

Taz's words froze Imani in the doorway.

". . . You right. Imani can't do nothing with me when I get good and ready. I got her back in check. She'll be in the studio working her tail off like always."

The sound of the tray crashing to the floor and the glass shattering made Taz yank the cell away from his ear. He looked up at Imani. "Now see . . . hold up girl. It wasn't like it sounded."

"Get out!"

"Biggie, later man." Taz waved the cell phone around trying to explain. "Imani, I was just talking to my boy. You know how it is, one brah talking to another brah, just talking a little garbage . . ."

"Get out!" Imani grabbed Taz's clothes and threw them out of her room into the kitchen area. "Now."

Taz followed his clothes and began putting them on, hopping around. "This floor is cold!"

Imani grabbed his K-Swisses and threw them at Taz's head. "Get out!"

"Quit it, girl! C'mon, Imani. Don't hate."

"Don't hate?"

"Yeah. I mean, act like, you know. Tell me you don't sit up and talk all kinds of junk when you're on the phone with one of your girls?"

Imani wouldn't say a word. She just pointed at the door.

Taz had his shoes and pants on now. *"Please,* that is not just a jock thing. I know y'all are up in that beauty shop talking mad gossip to each other just like we do in the locker room.

Shari's House of Style could be called Shari's House of Talking Shit!"

Imani snatched the door open, stared Taz down, and refused to either speak or blink.

He leaned in close and whispered, "You never brag to Shari that we turned each other out? Or that you have your man in check, that you have me in control under the sheets?"

"No." Imani growled, then pinched an inch of air. "Because I never wanted to tell her how little it was."

Then she slammed the door in Taz's face.

Chapter Sixteen

Time can open doors or close them. The space behind those doors is like a landscape where each individual's personality and morals grow.

Biggie faced Mr. Watson now. He watched as his mentor listened while playing with the medallion he kept on the end of a gold chain. It would be the first time that Biggie argued with a direct order. "It's not Maceo, Mr. Watson. Swear to God. It's that damn insurance company."

"Biggie. I like Maceo. Would any other mother be walking if they owed me the kind of money that he does?"

"No."

"He's got to get a message, Biggie. Like the mailman. Well, like I said, I like Maceo, so not *just* like that, just a little scare or something. Otherwise my rep won't be worth a pissed-on paper bag. Am I right or am I right?"

Biggie winced. "So you want me to reach out to him?"

"No son, I wouldn't do you like that. I wouldn't put that kindah pressure on you 'cause I know how loyal you are to your family, friends, and to me. Naw, I don't want you to do nothing."

Biggie sighed with relief. Then his eyes got wide with realization.

He started to speak.

"Hush, Biggie. I already sent Claude."

Imani sat in front of the candle and read the practice diction lines then ended with the scale. "A-E-I-O-U!"

"All right, Imani. You've been on fire the last couple of weeks. Your breath control is good. You're hardly using any slang. What's going on?"

"I guess I'm just ready for a change, Hops." Imani stood and stretched. She looked down and saw the papers on the desk. She read quickly. "Speaking of change." She picked up the top letter. "What's this?"

Hopson grabbed at the paper. "Give me that."

Imani turned away. "No. It's a job offer from Harvard. You're leaving, Hops?"

He grabbed the letter. "No I'm not. I get letters of interest from them and other schools like Michigan all the time. They're trying to recruit me."

"And you're sure you're not going to take it?"

"Who can say? More money. Better facilities. More prestige. Chairman Perkins is always riding me here. I'd be lying if I didn't admit that it's tempting."

A worried look crossed Imani's face.

"But not as tempting as my protégée. You're my focus, Imani. Forget about this other stuff. I'm not going anywhere."

Imani felt reassured. "Good."

"Now, did you listen to the tapes like I told you to?"

"Yes."

"Okay, let's go over here to the piano and try a little bit of it." Hopson sat at the piano and began to play. "Pretty, isn't it?"

"Hmm-huh."

"Oh, before I forget." He handed Imani an envelope with cash in it. "Here's your pay plus a little bonus."

"Two hundred dollars? Cool. We need it bad too."

"Not half as bad as we need to work on this song. Try the first line. Remember now, this love song is about missing someone . . . so it's soft and kind of mournful. Got it?"

Imani began to sing—

"Stop, stand up straight. Pretend you have a mike, and place your hands like I showed you."

Imani did.

"Good; very elegant. Now sing."

Imani felt awkward and her voice was strong but a bit flat.

Hopson got up. He stood behind her and circled his arms around her waist, then moved his hands up two inches. "The power is from here. Breath control. C'mon, breathe with me . . . now let it go . . . in and out."

Imani relished Hopson's touch.

Suddenly he stopped and stepped away. "Got it?"

Imani missed his touch. "Yeah, uh-huh. Got it."

Hopson sat back down at the piano. "Again from the top."

Imani assumed the position and began to sing. This time her voice was full and on point. Hopson played, smiling at her all the while.

Imani went flat again.

"No. You're not concentrating. Focus. And please don't improvise the notes. I wrote the song and I know how it should be sung."

"But putting some spin on that high note at the end of the phrase will give the song some flavor."

"Leave the flavor in the chicken shack. The song is perfect the way it is. Sing it like I tell you, Imani, and you'll bring the house down."

"What house?"

"Didn't I tell you? You're going to be performing at the charity ball at the president's mansion. Saturday. May eighth."

"That big chi-chi-pooh-pooh thing they have every year? When we were kids, me and Shari . . ."

"Shari and I."

"Shari and I used to climb the fence and watch the fancy cars bringing in all the black folks wearing tuxedos and long dresses."

"That's the chi-chi-pooh-pooh one all right."

"I'm performing there? How? Why?"

"Because you're talented and there's always a featured singer." Hopson let his fingers roll along the keys, playing pretty high notes. "Can you do it?"

Imani looked a little worried. "I don't know."

Hopson played a bass line fit for a horror movie. He joked menacingly, *"Suddenly fear washes over Imani's face. She sees a monster, and it's her own insecurity!"*

"Stop teasing."

"What?" Hopson switched to a ragtime tune. "The only thing blocking you is you."

"But . . ." Imani ran her hands over her sweatshirt and jeans. "All those women had such pretty dresses."

"So will you."

"How, Hops? I didn't think to save any of the money I've been making. I've been giving it all to my father. The insurance company is giving us a hard time and we're trying to fix up the club so we can at least reopen the stage area and bring some performers in."

Hopson jumped up and went over to his desk.

"What's wrong?"

"Class is over."

"Why, Hops?"

"Because you need to shop for a dress." He began writing out a check.

"I can't take that." Imani turned away, embarrassed that she didn't have the clothes, or the money to get a dress herself.

Hopson smiled at the pride this young diva possessed. He walked over to Imani and showed her the check. "I know you by now. Look at the memo line. It says: Loan. I'll take it out of your pay, say twenty-five dollars at a time."

She stared at the check.

"C'mon, Imani. Take it. I feel like Billy Dee Williams in that old movie *Lady Sings the Blues*." He quoted, " *'Take it before my arm falls off!'* "

Imani took it, quickly turned, grabbed her bag, and rushed out the door. Tears formed in her eyes as she whispered to herself, "I think I'm falling in love with you, Hops."

Chapter Seventeen

Falling in love is not just sensual, it's universal and happens to us in many different ways at different times in our lives. We fall in love with friends, with teachers. With people who show us kindness, faith, and parental guidance the way Maceo treated Taz, the lonely kid down the block who loved music. Taz had fallen in love with Maceo and risked his life now to help save him from Claude.

Maceo had gotten rotten drunk at the pool hall. He managed to stagger down the street and make it back inside his own club. He was so drunk that while he was outside, he waved to people he didn't know . . . pushed on the door when it said Pull . . . and when someone he knew asked, "How's your daughter?" Maceo answered, "I don't know, look like rain to me."

That had been three hours ago. Taz shook him hard as he snored with his head down on the bar. "Maceo! Get up! You gotta get out of here now."

He answered groggily, "Why?"

Biggie had managed to wait until Mr. Watson got on the phone. Then he called Taz and told him the deal.

"Can't you just go 'cause I say? Get up." Taz slung one of

Maceo's arms across his shoulders. He pushed up with his legs. "Maceo, you heavy as hell for an old man."

"That's all those collard greens and ham hocks on my bones."

"And your breath too! You need Scope."

"I need a drink," Maceo laughed and grabbed the bottle with his free hand. "My luck has got to change. I owe so much money it's a low-down dirty shame! Taz, don't tell nobody, but I'm broke."

"Don't tell nobody? Man, please."

"Don't tell nobody I can't pay."

"You're gonna pay with a body part in a minute if you don't shut up and come on here." Taz began walking Maceo towards the back door where he had parked his car. "And you need to go on a diet too, man."

Taz struggled with the door while trying to hold up Maceo. Taz reached and reached for the door, straining and sweating . . .

Suddenly the door crashed open knocking them both backwards onto the floor.

Splinters of wood wafted through the air and the busted lock now hanging on by a single screw swung back and forth. Claude stood flat-footed on the crushed doorframe and grinned. "Going somewhere, Taz?"

"Yeah. We, uh, we . . . we have an appointment."

"With who?" Maceo slurred.

"A doctor," Claude grunted.

"Claude, man, hold up. The money is coming. It's just taking a little more time than we thought. Biggie knows the deal."

Claude lunged forward, grabbing Taz by the collar, yanking him to his feet. "Biggie fights all your battles, punk? And what kind of a name is Taz anyway?"

He slapped Taz across the face before he could answer.

Taz spit blood. But didn't flinch. "Biggie gave me the name Taz, short for the Tasmanian Devil, my favorite cartoon character. And no, he don't fight all my battles for me. And I don't see why you wanna beat up an old man."

"You gonna stop me?"

Taz shrunk down. "No."

Claude began to loosen his grip. "That's what I thought."

"Leave him alone!" Maceo shouted. Fear was beginning to sober him up.

Claude glanced down at him and that's when Taz snapped his head back and let loose with a vicious head butt. Claude let go, staggered back, and grabbed his forehead just as a trickle of blood began running across his fingers. He grinned with delight.

"Oh God," Taz moaned. "I wish I haddah went to church on Sunday."

Claude brought his bloody hand down and then . . . licked it. *"Any Sunday!"*

Claude stepped forward and punched Taz in the stomach, dropping him to his knees. Spit formed in the corners of his mouth and he grabbed Claude's legs, locking his arms around them.

Claude grinned and sent two thunderous body punches into Taz's shoulders.

Taz felt his arms go dead from the elbow down. Claude stepped back and let Taz fall on his face, then Taz heard the click of a switchblade popping open.

Claude leaned down and sported the blade. "Punk, I'm gonna cut you every way but loose."

"Stop, Claude!"

He and Taz both looked towards the front doorway. Biggie was standing there.

"Who you giving orders to? You don't boss me."

"No," Mr. Watson said, stepping out from behind Biggie. "But I do."

Pure disappointment washed over Claude's face. He mumbled, "Damn."

Biggie raced over to Taz and helped him up. "You okay?"

Taz nodded. Next Biggie helped Maceo up off the floor and into a chair.

"Maceo, Biggie here has come up with an idea. Now the insurance money you'll be getting will cover fixing up the club and your initial debt—but not the interest."

"But didn't Taz tell ya? That insurance adjuster is giving me the flux."

"Not for long, Maceo." A sly grin spread across Mr. Watson's face.

Maceo cut his eyes towards Biggie.

"Now, like I was explaining, Biggie here suggested that you sign over to me half interest in Club Maceo to cover the current interest until you reopen."

"Give up part of my club?" Maceo wiped his mouth. He thought about it long and hard, before cradling his face in his hands. "Oh, God no. I've worked too long and too hard."

"Listen, Maceo," Mr. Watson said in a hard voice, "everybody's going out of their damn way for you. Taking chances for you. Biggie set that fire so you could get the insurance money."

"What!" Maceo was stunned for two seconds. Then he lunged at Biggie and tried to grab him by the collar. Biggie grabbed his hands in midair, forcing them down. "Wasn't me. It was Taz."

Maceo's jaw dropped. Slowly he turned in a stunned stupor. "Boy?"

"I had to, Maceo." Taz's eyes were sorry. "It was the only thing I could think of. I made sure you and Imani weren't nowhere around. Biggie helped me cover up afterwards. We're all trying to fix this thing. Can't you see that, man?"

Maceo slumped down into a nearby chair.

Biggie played the tough role. "Taz is on point, Maceo. Giving up part of the club is your only option, man. Turn this down and I wash my hands of it."

Claude jumped in. "But Mr. Watson, what you want with this broke-down old piece of club anyhow? Huh?"

"Let me explain, Claude. Once this club is fixed up, we'll have a grand opening. I hear all the kids around here talking about how talented Taz and Imani are. I'm a soul man myself but I know rap can make big bucks. If they perform at the grand opening, along with some more acts, and a buzz gets going, this club will be a moneymaking machine."

"Damn right." Biggie glared at Claude. "And what did I tell you about getting in my business?"

They lunged at each other. Mr. Watson stepped between them. Just his mere presence backed up both of the young bucks. "These boys got fire. Both of them. They just need to stop directing it at each other. Now, back to business. Whatya say, Maceo? We got a deal?"

Maceo was silent.

"I said do we have a deal?!"

Maceo nodded yes.

"Taz?"

"Deal."

That evening the men sealed their deal. The next day Shari and Imani were dealing with the tough task of finding a killer dress for the ball.

"Imani, all this shopping we gotta do would drive the average sistah nuts." Shari took her best friend by the arm. "But not me, girlie. I'm down with the program."

Imani and Shari were walking along the upscale shopping strip called Golden Heights. The streets were lined with all the high-end stores like Lord & Taylor and Bloomingdale's. Plus there was a slew of specialty boutiques.

Shari had *insisted* that they get in their finest for this shopping occasion. They were what folks in the 'hood called *clean* but actually their clothes were too hip, too tight, and made them stand out more than if they had just come dressed in a nice sweater and jeans.

"Shari, have you been shopping over here before? I've only passed by on the bus. Now I know why. These prices are *high.*"

"You've gotta pay the price to look boss, baby girl. I roll through here all the time," Shari lied. "I'm sure you can catch a sale."

"I'd better. Remember I want something—"

"Elegant and ladylike. *Please.* I remember what those women looked like. I was sitting on that fence with you, remember?"

"I know, girl."

"Then act like you know. Plus would I let my best girlfriend show up at the ball looking like a skeezer?"

"No." Imani smiled. "I'm glad you came with me, girl."

"You know Shari gotcha back."

"Good. Let's hit Bloomingdale's first. Which way?"

"Uh-uh." Shari looked confused. "I think over there."

"Thought you shopped here all the time, Miss Big Baller."

"Yeah, yeah, girl. You know I get turned around in my own house. Chill. There it is, over there."

The store clerks turned their noses up at the two around-the-way girls, hardly wanting to show them any dresses. This happened in store after store.

Shari was mad as a trapped lion. "If one more of those *uppity store clerk hos* gives me attitude, I'm gonna snatch her hair out by the roots!"

Imani was near tears.

"Girl, don't cry. We'll find a dress. And you're gonna be slamming. *Just slamming.*"

"Think so?"

"Know so. Listen. Obviously these store skeezers don't know

how to treat nobody. And, quiet as it's kept, if you buy something around here you still might see somebody else at the ball with the same thing on anyway."

Imani leaned back on a building and shook her head.

"So let's take that money and buy some material and have my girlfriend Rita make you a dress."

"Rita sews?"

"Girl, yeah. She's in her second year of design school. She'll help us pick out the material and the patterns, everything."

Imani was unsure, but she didn't want to face another rude store clerk. "Okay. When do you think we can go?"

"Sunday. The salon is closed. Speaking of, I need to be getting back there now with a quickness. Those hot-curling mamas will walk out with the dryers if I'm not there to close up."

"Okay, Shari. That's cool. I have to get over to the university to see Hops anyway." Imani smiled at the thought.

"Aww, look out now. Don't be a fool and fall in love with the man."

"I'm not."

"You sure? Ain't nothing up between y'all?"

Imani shrugged.

"Listen, girl. He's uptown and you're downtown. An uptown man only wants a downtown girl for one thing, to play. They not trying to make you their wife or have you on their arm showing the world that you're their woman. You are from two different worlds. Two different backgrounds. He'll never think you're good enough. The world will never let you think you're good enough."

"Stop. Just stop already," Imani growled. She cracked, hoping to hide her growing affection for the professor. "What would I want with his corny butt anyway? Huh? He's not fly. How would he play on the low end?"

Her best friend laughed at the thought of it.

"Shari, I just want this to be perfect, you know? Most of all because of how we used to watch those women going to the ball and pretend like we were one of them."

Shari hugged Imani. "And this time we will be one of them— it'll be you, Imani. You, girl. And you're gonna represent for all the downtown Cinderellas."

Chapter Eighteen

All Cinderella wanted to do was go to the ball. She didn't have to be queen of the ball or stay until the very end. Her dream was just to go and fit in with everyone else, to be one of the cool and smooth crowd, to hang and have folks let her hang.

That's how Dee felt, like the abused campus Cinderella who just wanted to fit in with her peers. Dee was mousy-looking with thick glasses, and she played in the horn section next to Ahmad. Dee never missed a change or hit a bad note on a complicated number. Despite Dee's talent, the cool folks in the band, especially Ahmad, ignored her outside of rehearsal. They never asked her to come hang at the student union with them or off campus at the Spoken Word coffeehouse. Never.

And so when Dee saw Ahmad heading for his car, she ran to catch up hoping that he would invite her to hang, see that she was cool too. But what could she say to get his attention? What did she know that was interesting?

Dee told Ahmad about how she was walking by Professor Hopson's office and overheard him arguing with Chairman Perkins. To her joy, *Ahmad was listening!* He couldn't take his eyes off her. Ahmad actually stopped walking, pulled her close, and put his arm around her shoulders lending her his ear.

Dee told him about Imani. The bet. How it would play out for Professor Sherman. Ahmad swore her to secrecy and of course Dee promised. Now could she hang out with him? Of course she could, Ahmad said. Wait here at the car, I'll be right back.

Professor Sherman was cutting-edge. He believed in using computer technology in music. Often he'd have some of his more talented students record tracks for a system he called looping. Professor Sherman would have, say, a violinist record a song three different times in various keys—then he'd loop them over at strategic times giving the effect of a gospel choir's call and refrain. With a computer program he perfected, he could get it down to half a note while making multiple edits at once. That's what Professor Sherman had written his research paper on. He hoped to submit it for the grant competition.

Sherman was in the music studio with the computer sound system he had rigged up and was playing with a couple of tracks when Ahmad came in and said he had some interesting news. Although it was only the two of them in the studio, Ahmad felt the need to almost whisper, forcing Professor Sherman to lean forward.

What Professor Sherman heard made him fall back in his seat. He thought long and hard. "Don't tell anyone else, okay, Ahmad?"

"Sure, Professor Sherman. But what are you going to do about it?"

"Nothing."

"Why?"

"Because I don't think Hopson can pull it off. Make that around-the-way girl a throaty diva? No way. But you keep your ears open for me, Ahmad. I'm going to be watching too. I don't know why but something tells me I need to keep an eye on the competition."

*   *   *

Sometimes what you don't know really *will* hurt you. Like the insurance adjuster who was out to take yet another look at Club Maceo to try to determine if the fire was an accident or arson—*what he didn't know really would hurt him.*

He didn't know that when he arrived at the club, the owner, Maceo, wasn't going to be there.

The insurance adjuster thought he had the old man's number . . . figured that Maceo had the fire set to get his hands on a juicy claim. But the arson job was a good one; it looked suspicious but wasn't clear-cut enough for the city fire department to rule it a crime and not an accident. So it was up to him as an adjuster to stall and get a private investigator in or lowball the award damages before canceling the policy outright.

But what the insurance adjuster didn't know was that Maceo and his new partner would send their representatives to meet him. Biggie and Taz were lying in wait.

Biggie yanked the insurance adjuster by the collar, threw him up against the wall, and braced him there with a forearm to the chest. The insurance adjuster's feet were three inches off the ground, his arms dangling like meat on a slaughterhouse hook. Biggie growled. "What's your problem, man?"

The insurance adjuster wanted to answer but right about now he was real short on air.

"Biggie, jack him up, brah. This guy's been dissin' Maceo like crazy, holding up the insurance money. All that. He ain't right, Biggie."

The insurance adjuster's eyes widened with fear.

"My dog Taz here says you ain't right. So I guess I gotta straighten you out." Biggie eased the pressure of the hold.

"Way-way—," the adjuster panted.

"You trying to say 'wait'?" Biggie asked.

"Making us wait is why you're in trouble now," Taz shouted. "You're the one who's been jamming up our claim. And for what? It's not like it's your money."

Biggie eased the pressure on the insurance adjuster's chest so he could speak.

"It's my job. They're on us all day about all the big claims in this area, telling us to find ways *not* to pay out."

Biggie shook the insurance man like a rag doll.

"Listen, you squash this arson talk and get everything together and on point. 'Cause that old man you've been stalling has backup now. Mr. Watson is the new co-owner, and he's the baddest cat on the low end. So you better put that report through and have them cut us a check by the end of the week or I'm out looking for your ass."

"Okay, okay." Big pellets of sweat were beading across the insurance man's brow. "Whatever you want."

Biggie tossed him towards the door. "Then get on the ball, niggah."

Taz laughed as the man ran away. "Hey, did you hear him, Biggie? Wanted to know if it was arson. Damn right it was. Maceo needed the money. Bet that guy would have pissed himself if he knew I was the one who set it and I'm standing right here in front of him, huh? That's kindah funny ain't it?"

A woman's gurgle and then her gasp erupted behind them. Biggie and Taz turned and saw Imani standing there. Anger and hurt made her hands fly to her lips.

"Aww damn," Taz cursed under his breath.

Imani spun around and ran out the door.

Taz started to run after her.

"Wait, dog. She's hurt. Where's she gonna go? Nowhere but to Shari's house. Give her a minute to get a grip. And take a second to get your mind right. 'Cause tonight you're gonna have to really talk to your woman."

Taz found Imani at Shari's house. She didn't want to talk. She wanted to pack.

"C'mon, Imani. Calm down."

"Calm down? What for, Taz? So you can lie to me. If I don't calm down, then what? Are you going to burn this house down too?"

"See? Stupid stuff. You always talk stupid stuff when you get mad. I never lied to you about setting that fire. When did you ask me about it, huh? When?"

"Don't trip, Taz. How would I know to ask you that? All this time I've been mad at Biggie, thinking he did it, and it was you all along."

"What was I supposed to say, girl? '*I know Biggie didn't set the fire 'cause I did. Biggie just came up on me after I set it and helped me throw away the evidence. He ran into you by accident.*' Is that what I was supposed to say?"

"Something like that, yes."

"Imani, get real, please."

"And what makes it worse, Taz, you were punk enough to let me be suspicious of him all this time when *you* knew he didn't do it."

"Punk? You calling me a punk? This *punk* standing here put his life on the line for *your* daddy. Maceo owes big money."

"What? To who? For what?"

"Aww, see there, girl. You've got me so pissed off that I'm talking crazy. Forget that. Just forget it."

"How can I? And you're crazy, but not that crazy. Don't play with me when it comes to my daddy."

Taz sighed heavily. "All right. Maceo owes Mr. Watson some serious cheddar. He started gambling—"

"But he promised!"

"And he stopped. The man slipped up. He's cool now, but the interest has been piling up on his debt. I've been killing myself trying to figure out ways to help Maceo."

"*Some help,* lying to me about all this mess."

"I am some help. Maceo was about to get beat down by Claude and I stepped in. Me. Taz. Not Mister University Man."

"Stop lying."

"Girl, I'm about an inch off you. Stop calling me a lie every two seconds."

"Then stop lying every two seconds."

Taz gritted his teeth and grabbed Imani by the arm. She glared at him. "What's your next move? Are you going to throw me up against the wall like Biggie did the insurance man?"

He let her arm go. "I can't hit you. I can't hurt you. And damn if I ain't having a hard time loving you right about now. And you wanna know why? 'Cause you're changing up on me, Imani. Look at you. You talking funny and you acting funny."

"How am I acting funny, Taz? By not jumping when you call? For not running to the studio because you say? Because I want something better for myself?"

"Naw, because you're acting like something you're not. Imani, you're not uptown. You'll always be a downtown girl. That's real. If you wanna run from me? That's cool. Run on." Then Taz leaned forward and gave Imani a peck on the cheek. "But baby, please, don't run away from yourself."

Where do we flee when something we trust breaks? We flee to what is sturdy, hoping *whatever* it is . . . or *whoever* it is . . . will be strong enough to give shelter. So Imani packed her things and wound up on Professor Hopson's doorstep.

She had no idea what he would do or what he would say, this man who had helped her see another side of herself. They had begun to rehearse some of the songs that Hopson wanted her to sing at the ball.

He showed her things about breath control, about style, about being a diva in presence but not in attitude. The songs he picked were beautiful, yet he arranged them with difficult key changes, which, when pulled off, made the song sound brilliant.

Imani hadn't sung much, so she never really knew the range and the power of her own voice. She hadn't sung much because her own mother's voice rang so clear in her memory: a mother gone too soon from heart failure and a failed music career.

So Imani chose rap—not singing like her mother or playing an instrument like her father. Choice sometimes gives us room to find ourselves. This choice had helped Imani the girl, but now she was Imani the woman and she saw that she had more depth, more music in her, and that all of it was bursting to get out.

The man who had released this feeling inside of her was not her lover, Taz, or her father, Maceo, but a professor who saw it in her when she could not see it in herself.

And Imani loved Hopson for having that vision, for dreaming a dream for her. She waited now on the doorstep, waiting, occasionally looking up at the light still on in his study, and she wondered.

We wonder about the places where we will plant our seeds of love. Is it the right ground? Is it fertile ground? How much tending must be given to it? How much will be returned? Will it sprout prematurely and then die? Will it flower in full bloom one season and then disappear totally the next?

Imani hesitated, then found courage. She rang the doorbell and waited. She heard his steps, which had a slow plodding sound similar to the one her heart was beating out inside her chest. Imani imagined his hand on the doorknob as he looked through the peephole. If he answered quickly, turned the lock hard, it would be okay. That meant that he saw her, knew she was in trouble, and immediately wanted to help. If he hesitated, Imani told herself, then turned the lock slowly, he didn't really care.

Imani heard the lock flick and make a loud thud and when Hopson opened the door and reached for her without hesitation, her heart leapt with joy.

"What are you doing out this time of night? It's dangerous, not to mention storming."

Hopson saw her suitcase.

"Hops, I need a place to stay. Everything's crazy, just crazy . . . Please."

"Please what? Of course you can stay here. C'mon in. Dry off. Warm up. Besides, I have a surprise for you."

Imani came in, wrapped in a combination of awkwardness and insecurity. Hopson took her things to a guest bedroom, gave her a towel, and told her to get out of her wet things while he made some tea.

"What's the surprise?"

"I'm not telling yet. But from the looks of you, you could use a nice surprise."

Imani took a hot shower, the water rushing against her skin, massaging the strained nerves. The flowing drops cascading down her back tickled, and she closed her eyes and thanked God that she had found this place tonight, a place away from everything else she had known. Strange, this place, yet comforting; she could take time to think, to understand everything that was happening to her.

Imani dried off and grabbed a big, comfy cotton robe that she had packed. She wanted to wait a few minutes before getting dressed and going downstairs. Imani laid out on the bed and stretched, her heartbeat finally settling down as she began to relax. The soft drumming of the rain could be heard against the window. She fought the drowsiness that tried to overcome her.

Then Imani heard it.

The horn that blew twilight notes that danced on the ceiling and wafted down on her body.

It was a twilight sound that found its way beneath her skin and broke her out of a state of temporary comfort, jolting her upright. Imani walked forward, hardly able to feel the bottoms of her feet, bare and slightly damp, as they left a ghostly impression against the hardwood floors behind her.

How quickly she moved, her heart in her throat, crowding

the vocal chords, freezing them solid like a cold Chicago breeze. By the time she reached the common area from which the sound came, her eyes were filled with tears.

There was Hopson with the tea on the table, grinning at her. "Surprise!" he said.

Imani drew her hands to her lips.

"Joe lost your cell number so he called me instead. He said you wanted this album. I went and got it for you. I bought it as a gift, since you've been working so hard."

Her father's horn intro had given way to the sound of her mother's voice. It swirled around Imani like a wind. Slowly, the first tear began to fall from her eyes.

"What's the matter, Imani?"

She shook her head, unable to speak.

Hopson rushed over to her, held her. "Why the tears? Whatever it is can't be that bad, can it?"

"That's my mother. That was the only album she ever made. We lost the only copies we had in the fire."

"But you never told me your mother was a jazz singer, just that your father played and arranged."

Imani nodded.

"But why?"

"I didn't want any comparing. I didn't want you to assume that I could sing just because my mother was a jazz singer. I wanted to see what you thought of me on my own."

"Imani, your mother has a beautiful voice. And you have a beautiful voice. What you do with your gift is up to you and God. Nobody else. Now, come on. Sit down. And if you feel like it, you can tell me about your mother."

The best listeners hear with their hearts.

Hopson, wearing jeans and a T-shirt, sat facing Imani, who was on the couch, her legs curled beneath her. Her hair was wet and laid softly all around her brow. Imani's nose was two shades of Rudolph red. She sniffled twice before sipping the herbal tea he had warmed for her.

They listened to the entire album.

Then Imani told him about her mother and other things too. And Hopson listened with his heart.

This was the seed.

Chapter Nineteen

The natural place for a seed is in the ground. So it is only fitting that another word for ground is *foundation,* as in *sturdy start,* as in *a solid base.*

Imani and Hopson's foundation would not be in possessions of the world, the *bling-bling* of knowing that one person is high profile and carrying a lot of money and the other person is trying to ride, trying to get a grip on the comforts and suck up the spoils.

And neither would they find their foundation in the twist of the sheets, *i.e., the skins, baby,* that came with passionate tiptoeing in the midnight hour, lusting for the touch of one hot body against another—*whether those bodies belonged to each other in the daylight or not.*

No, their foundation would be developed slowly and built rather frailly. They would tell each other things that they had chosen before to keep to themselves. Not always things embarrassing or secretive, but just notions and hopes and ideas.

It was not necessarily in the telling that they found a bridge, but in the reception. When Imani spoke to Hopson in their intimate talks, her words were suns bursting inside his ears. It had gotten to be like that. When Hopson spoke to Imani, his words were a string of light dancing on her eardrums.

Conversation, simple and pure, is so underrated in what connects two people to each other. High marks are checked off in the world for good looks, for having money, or education, or charm. But the ability to exchange streams of thoughts about ordinary things had become an extraordinary thing in a world of e-mails, Post-it notes, chat rooms with windows but no walls, and "holler" pages from one beeper to another.

Imani watched him one day, playing a piece he had written. He wore baggy sweats and a half-cut-off T-shirt. He was hitting all the notes but the emotion was as bare as tree branches in the fall. Imani could tell that he was struggling. And in his struggle she felt something sensual, the way he contorted his torso and pushed the wind into the horn that extended from his body like a third arm, flapping around in hopes of grabbing something to squeeze and caress.

Imani whispered, "Play it again, Hops. But this time through me." And Imani closed her eyes and stretched her body out, letting it fall loose and limp.

And he gazed at Imani and somehow understood, though this experience would be totally new to him. Like a charmer he began to play as if he were inside her. He felt the curve of her hips that moved slowly to his song; felt them from the inside out, pumping with the blood that on up-tempo riffs rolled like rapid water against the shores of her skin and bone.

Down-tempo he cruised through the soft part of her mouth, slowly winding beneath her tongue that had often filled a lover's mouth.

The ending low note landed beneath the palms of Imani's hands and made them clutch uncontrollably, squeezing rhythm's fruit until it was driven out of her body in the form of moist drops that beaded around the horn's metal lips.

Near exhaustion, Hopson slid into a nearby chair and quietly demanded, "Now you."

And Imani smiled at him and began to sing one of her songs

through him. She found the exact spot she wanted with her very first note, a single simple word: "You."

That spot was next to his heart, a difficult place to reach. But she held that first note drilling it against his rib cage looking for an opening to slip through the way sun rays find openings in the clouds.

Once there, his body, unlike hers, didn't allow Imani to roam free. His body fought back, flesh grabbing at her melody, using it like extra blood that ballooned his temples and swelled his maturity.

But she moved. Nothing could hold her as she moved and warmed all his insides through and through like a smoking ghost. He could barely stand it, eyes closed, sweat pouring off his body.

The ending high note seemed to rise to the top of Hopson's skull, filling the inside of his brain, swimming around against the system that controls the body's nerves. Imani held the note as long as she could, then stopped before she would drown, emerging above his surface satisfied and gasping for air.

They had found their fit musically, but where else would that lead?

"Girl, you are headed for a world of trouble." Maceo was cold sober. His hot stare burned all around Imani. "Called Shari's looking for you. Her mother answered the phone. She said you had quit working at the shop and had moved out and was staying over at the university."

Imani mumbled, "Ma June talks too much."

"Entirely too much," Maceo agreed. "But she sure said a mouthful this time. Who you staying with over there?"

Imani was silent. She was irritated too. She hated it when her father played this game: asking questions he knew the answer to.

"I'm staying with a friend, Daddy."

"Who you know in college? What girlfriend you got that's staying on campus?"

"Daddy, just say what you've got to say, please."

"You damn right I'm gonna say what I've got to say." He lit a cigarette. "And how I wanna say it too. What you doing staying with that strange man?"

"You make him sound all creepy. He's not a serial killer or something."

"Could be. I don't know nothing about the man. Neither do you."

"He's a professor. He's smart. He's talented. He found Mama's album."

"And I appreciate that. Lord knows I do. But that don't give him dibs on you, does it? I still don't know nothing about him hardly."

"What else do you need to know, Daddy? His people are from Georgia. They own Leroy Oil."

"I don't care if they own Standard Oil and got pumps in their backyard. I don't like you living with this man, just like that." Maceo snapped his fingers.

"Well what did you want me to do?" Imani's lip quivered. "I had nowhere else to go."

"Huh?" Maceo bit down on the tip of the cigarette and nearly split it in two. "You could have stayed where you were . . ."

"Daddy . . ."

"Or you could have gone to one of your other girlfriends'. You got plenty of friends, Imani."

"I don't want to have to explain to anybody. I don't want to have to keep hearing Shari ask me how come I hardly come by the shop anymore."

"That's a fair question."

"And Taz telling me I talk funny or Ma June constantly asking me how it's going and getting in my business whenever she can. I don't want to have to explain why I'm trying something new—why I'm feeling different."

"Whatcha trying to say, Imani?"

"My old crew. My old ways. They don't feel like me anymore."

"And that persnickety campus that you've been on for 'bout two seconds is now you?"

"That doesn't feel like me altogether either. Something is happening and I'm not sure what it is, Daddy. But it's something and I don't want to have to try and explain what I can't explain. I just want to be with someone who understands that I'm going through something and it's okay."

"And that's him. That professor boy?"

"Yeah, Daddy. He's helping me musically and we talk about things outside of music. Books. What's happening in the news."

"I watch CNN," Maceo grunted. "I know how to hold a conversation. I'm no booga bear."

Imani put her arms around her father's neck. "You're growling like one *right now.*"

Maceo fought the urge to smile. "Separate bedrooms?"

"Yes."

"I still don't like it. But you're grown."

Thank God, Imani thought.

"As soon as the upstairs is livable, you come home just like we planned. I'm not gonna bother you about this thing or this mood you're going through. I just wanna be sure you're safe."

"I am, Daddy."

"You watch him."

"Okay."

"You tell him I got a shotgun."

Imani laughed.

"A loaded shotgun, and unless he wants another hole in his ass he'll behave."

"I will."

"I still don't understand why you had to leave Shari's."

Imani shrugged.

"And you stopped speaking to Taz altogether. Is something else bothering you? What's going on?"

Imani swallowed. "I have something to tell you."

"Is it that bad? You oughtah see the look on your face, baby."

Imani forced a fake smile. It was pitiful.

"Oh Lord, what's the matter now?"

"I think you oughtah know, Daddy. But I don't wanna hurt you."

"Let me worry about that."

"It's about Taz. I overheard him and Biggie talking. It was Taz who set the fire."

"Oh," Maceo huffed out, then quickly turned away. "Well I'm sure he didn't mean no harm."

The words hit Imani like a fist. "Didn't mean no harm? Daddy?" Maceo looked at his daughter. She looked at him. "I can't fool you and you can't fool me. You knew."

"Imani . . ."

"Damn."

"Hush that now. Don't go flying off the handle like you do."

"You *did* know."

"He just told me."

"And you didn't *tell me?* I was going to tell you."

"The boy did it so we could get the insurance money. Insurance companies got plenty of money and God knows I've paid in more than my share and never claimed a dime before. So I'm due. We'd get that insurance money, fix this old place up, and then . . ."

". . . and then pay off the money you owe Mr. Watson. I know about that, too, Daddy. You broke your promise."

"Listen here, now, where do you get off being so high-handed?"

"From you, Daddy. You always talked about working hard and being honest. From you."

Maceo felt a rush of shame then quickly shook it off. "You

young folks don't understand that sometimes in life you have to cut corners and do things you wouldn't normally do."

"Okay, Daddy. Just give me some space. I—I just want some space for a while. Let me sort stuff out in my head. Can you give me that? Please?"

"All right, Imani. All right, child."

Maceo watched her go away without so much as a fuss. Instinct told him to let his daughter be.

Sometimes when we don't follow our instincts we're led to an awful place. Not awful like Dante's hell but to a place where we have no control over what happens around us.

Biggie's instinct told him not to go on this collection with Claude, although Mr. Watson had ordered them not to go around the projects alone. Something told him not to go, some kind of instinct.

I don't trust this niggah as far as I can throw his ugly ass, Biggie said to himself as he waited on the corner for Claude to pick him up. He still didn't know why Mr. Watson was insisting that they collect together in the projects. Nothing unusual had jumped off since he had beat down the mailman for pulling a pistol on him.

As Biggie waited, a bling-bling, rimmed out, silver-and-black Hummer Two turned the corner and headed his way. He didn't recognize the car. But clearly it belonged to a big baller. Biggie could see his mirrored reflection in the tinted windows. He fingered the gun in his waistband.

Biggie shrugged. He didn't fear death. Never had. In science class, neither the iced organs nor the preserved animals to dissect bothered him. Biggie knew what he was going to be in the world and knew what the consequences could be. People were always looking to take a shot at him; wanna-bes trying to make their bones, or has-beens who had gotten their ass kicked for not paying Mr. Watson his money. *So what?* Biggie always reasoned.

That's just how the game is played, how the street toughs roll. I'm Biggie and I'm still here.

He watched now as the window slowly rolled down.

Biggie eased his gun out.

"Get in. Or you wanna take the bus?" Claude yelled.

Biggie got in. "This thing is sweet. You got it rocking up in here, too, with all the upgrades. When did you get it?"

"Last week."

"This cost you some cheddar, Claude. A bare Hummer is fifty G's for the legit black businessman and seventy G's for a street hustler like you, who's upgraded it with all the toys."

"I gotta have a ride like this, man. I'm an up-and-coming brother of status."

"Stop popping off so much, man, and handle business."

"I'm just stating the obvious. I got juice and my ladies like to ride in style."

"What ladies, Claude? Those ugly biscuit-head girls you roll with?"

"Don't hate." Claude laughed. "Envy."

"Don't talk." Biggie shot back. "Drive."

Something told him not to go, despite Mr. Watson's orders. What is instinct anyway? A voice inside of you that aligns with the moon and gives you vision into what can be? Or is it whispers from the unknown trying to help us out down here on earth?

Whatever it is, Biggie played it off. *I ain't no punk,* he thought. *I'm gonna handle my business with this fool and be through.*

So they rolled up on the card game in the storage room of the project where five dollars got you in, but if you won more than a hundred dollars you couldn't get out.

"Take it easy, Claude."

"Easy is for babies and old bitches. Which are you?"

Biggie sneered behind his back.

Claude burst into the room and two men reached for their guns. Biggie was already down on one knee aiming with two guns. "One to hurt you and one to kill you. So I'd advise you motherfuckers not to pull a piece or nothing funny. Feel me?"

Claude spotted the man he wanted. He was a little man. He looked like the munchkin mayor in the *Wizard of Oz*. Claude cast an imposing shadow over the man when he barked out his demands.

"Where's Mr. Watson's money? I want it now."

A stunned look spread across the man's face. "Huh?"

Claude grabbed him by the back of the neck. "Where's the money?"

"I paid you. You know I paid you."

"Stop lying!" Then Claude began to punch and kick the man. "I paid. I paid."

Claude beat him more. A woman standing in the corner, a young girl, pretty and matured by the streets, backed the claim. "He did, though. He did pay. Swear to God he did."

Biggie heard her and framed her face with an edgy glance. Then he looked at the man's face. *They were telling the truth.* Biggie had been collecting too long. He knew how to read people. They were not lying. Suddenly a picture of the silver and black H2 flashed in his mind. Something told him not to come. Now Biggie knew what he didn't want to know: *Claude was stealing.*

Mr. Watson was like a father to Biggie, much in the way that Maceo had stepped up for Taz. That's why Biggie was trying so hard to help them out of the mess they were in. Biggie was fiercely loyal to Mr. Watson and as much as he couldn't stand Claude, he thought he was loyal too. Biggie made up his mind to do some digging. Claude was stealing; Biggie's gut said so. But what he needed now was concrete evidence.

Chapter Twenty

Meanwhile there was plenty of evidence that Hopson was making headway with Imani. Real headway. Professor Sherman had caught a glimpse of her rehearsing a couple times, after hours. And what Sherman saw made him nervous; so he decided to rattle Hopson's cage the very first chance he got. And that chance came when they ran into each other in the campus studio.

"Hey, man. I wondered when we'd bump into each other." Sherman was sitting in the music studio; he'd been editing some tracks on the computer. "You've been pretty busy, huh? With teaching and helping Imani and whatnot."

Hopson couldn't help but smile. The image of Imani singing flashed through his mind. She was making great strides, and he was now more confident than ever that he'd win the bet. "It's going well."

"Real well, *huh, Hops?*" Professor Sherman's words dripped with sarcasm.

"The name is Hopson." He realized that Professor Sherman had obviously been doing a bit of spying on him and Imani. "And what's your point?"

"*Sorry.* I just thought that since you've got a downtown

sistah shacking up with you, that uh-huh, you might suddenly be down. Thought you might want everybody to call you Hops."

"Why would I want that? And we're not shacking. She's in the guest room until she finds a place. After that she'll be out on her own, conquering the world with her talent."

"And that's it?" Sherman wasn't about to let on that he knew about the bet. But still he wanted to pick at him. "I think there's more to it than that."

"Like what?" Professor Hopson held his breath. Did he know about the bet?

"Do you like her?"

"Like her—" Hopson sputtered. "Like her, sure I like her."

"I mean, maybe deep down inside you want to get with her or something?"

Professor Hopson balked. "You talk like one of the students. 'Get with her.' That sounds so ghetto."

"Excuse me, Mister High Class. That's my low-end roots showing. Sorry."

"I didn't mean it like that, Sherman. Really . . ."

"No." Professor Sherman stood up. "Just be careful. That's all I've got to say."

"Sherman, wait a minute."

"I don't mind you feeling and acting superior sometimes around me. I really don't."

"C'mon, Sherman. We're friends."

"Because I *know* you're not superior. But this kid is from the low end. She's different. She needs help and you're giving it to her. Fine. But don't make her some kind of pet project then drop her like a hot potato. I'm from downtown and I know what this means to her."

"I'd never, ever do anything to hurt Imani. All I want to do is help her. Where's all this bullshit coming from?"

"It's not bullshit. Don't treat her like some downtown stereotype. I'm just saying if you're going to mentor her, do it right. Black folks owe that to each other. Understand?"

"Yeah, I understand. But why don't you take your own advice? Stop stereotyping *me*. You think because my family has money that I must be out of touch. That I can't understand. That I can't relate."

"How can you? C'mon, Hopson, get real. I mean, what's a rich boy like you know about downtown girls anyway, huh?"

"Sure, Imani is from downtown. People think the girls there have no class and no style. They think the girls just want some poor chump to take their money and give them babies. That's a bunch of crap. There are beautiful and talented people everywhere—black and white, rich and poor. Even right in the heart of the ghetto."

Sherman played devil's advocate. "And you know for sure that Imani's one of them?"

"Damn right."

"So you're falling for her? Sounds like you've got your nose open, Hopson."

"Sounds like you should mind your own damn business."

"C'mon, Hops. Don't be like that. We're just talking man to man. What's wrong with that? I mean, *you've gotta try her.*"

Hopson angrily turned to leave. Professor Sherman kept talking.

"A downtown girl like Imani is probably the bomb between the sheets. But hey, if you can't handle it, I'd be glad to step in and uh"—he made a fist and thrust the air—"ya know."

Hopson grabbed Sherman by the collar and pinned him back up against the wall. "Shut up before I ram my fist down your throat."

Sherman smiled. He smiled for two reasons. One, he saw the fire and the sincerity in Hopson's eyes. He really did care. And two, Sherman knew he could take Hopson at any moment, but he didn't.

"Now I'm talking man to *dog,* Sherman. Stay away from Imani. And when you talk about her? You talk about her with respect."

"Good for you, man." Sherman gently pushed his hands away. "Good for you."

"What?" Hopson was hopelessly confused.

"Professor, you're in love."

Hopson didn't know what to say. He just whirled around and stomped out of the studio.

"How's this, Maceo?" Taz yelled out, although he was only a few feet away from him. The workmen rehabbing the club were extraordinarily loud.

Maceo read the poster.

Club Maceo presents a Grand Opening Concert. Sat. May 8. Music by: Up-and-coming producer Taz & His Hip-Hop All-Stars. Headlining the night: Imani . . . the fastest-rising rapper on the scene, plus many more. Tickets: $20 in advance and $25 at the door. Club Maceo is completely remodeled and soon to be the hippest club in town.

Taz was grinning from ear to ear.

"That's an awful big smile, son."

"Can't help it. I'm just so happy we're finally about to get out from under I don't know what to do. We're about to get paid."

"I'm happy, too, Taz." Maceo paused then tilted his head. "But let me ask you something." He had only talked to his daughter briefly over the past few weeks and it was killing him not to discuss the concert, but Taz had insisted that Maceo leave the details to him. "You sure Imani is okay about this? I mean I know she's still mad at all of us."

"Didn't I tell you not to say anything to her about it? She'll be here. She'll be here rapping her guts out. I've got it all under control. Haven't I saved your butt before?"

"Yeah."

"Then trust, Maceo. Trust."

"But things are different this time. Watson is in play and there's no room for mess-ups. I'm trusting you, Taz. God knows you've been like a son to me. I just wish you and Imani would stop all the humbugging y'all do."

"Love her, but your daughter is crazy, Maceo."

"What woman isn't?"

Taz held his palm out and the two men slapped five sideways, *twice*. "Speak the truth, old man, speak the truth. I'm giving Imani some space and then once this concert kicks off . . . she'll see how good this club looks and what I can do. Then she'll be back digging on me like before. She'll be back down with the program, Maceo. Taz and Imani . . . together."

"Is that what you think? Or is that what you hope?"

The question caught Taz so much by surprise that his only response was dead silence.

In the silence of quiet times we allow ourselves to think about the things that are important to us. In quiet times we can sense the emotion that one person emits, and what effect it has on us.

Hopson had reached out to Imani and taken her in, not just because she had asked, but also because she was in need. He reached for her the way a sailor instinctively reaches for the man overboard even though it's dangerous for him.

The humanity is in the unselfish act of saving another.

Hopson and Imani stayed in separate rooms but shared a common goal: to get ready for the ball. The two worked feverishly on their songs, hours and hours on end late at night. They spent a great deal of time at his office, working on her vocal style.

Imani even began to get hoarse, until Hopson told her to drink herbal tea with honey and lemon; he also advised her to nurse the vocal chords at night with warm towels. Dinner for them was not just a meal but also a lesson. He showed Imani how the table settings would be at the ball with salad forks and soupspoons and flute glasses. He also put on a classical CD to show her ballroom dancing.

"C'mon, Hops. You're kidding, right? We'll be dancing to this dry music all night?"

They were in his office, late evening, and Imani was growing irritable with fatigue.

"Not all night, Imani. Here's the tradition. Just after the featured vocalist sings—that's you—a waltz is played for the patrons and other guests to dance to."

"Whatever! Let's get back to rehearsal. We're wasting time."

Hopson ignored her and went to the door after he heard a knock. It was Rome, the janitor.

"Evening, Professor. Y'all working late again I see."

"Yes we are."

"Hi, Mr. Rome." Imani yawned. They had met before on some of the other nights that she and Hops worked late.

"Hi, baby. I'm just gonna empty the wastebaskets and be out y'all way."

Hopson asked Imani, "Can you dance?"

"To this? Please. Now the second song needs some work—"

"No it doesn't. And let me see."

"See what, Hops?"

"If you know how to dance to a waltz."

"What's the matter? You think I'm gonna go *grinding around* on every man in the place and not be a lady?"

Rome cleared his throat twice, then chuckled. He cut his eyes at Hopson.

"I didn't say that." Hopson was grinning now. "I want to see. Let's dance."

Imani looked at him with a crooked smile. "I don't know about you, Professor."

Rome decided to help. "He's a good dancer."

"He is?"

"Yeah." Rome recalled the night he'd found Hopson dancing alone in his office. Rome pointed to the broom. "If you don't believe me, ask her."

Hopson growled, "Good-bye, Rome."

Rome shuffled out of the office, laughing to himself.

"What was that about?"

"Nothing. You know Rome." Hopson took Imani's hand and drew her close. The CD stopped. The couple was waiting for the next one to play.

The smell of her hair—his cologne—mingled together and began to awaken Hopson's sensibilities. Then he realized that something was wrong. *What is it?* he thought. Then he realized, for some reason, some strange reason, he was uncomfortable.

"Sorry, Imani. It'll just be a minute."

Imani drew herself closer. "Hush the rush. I could stand like this all day."

And her comments made him feel warm and wanted. Then the waltz began and they danced. Imani was a little awkward at first, only because he counted aloud for her, "One-two-three . . . One-two-three . . ."

Imani pressed her fingertips to his lips. "Sssh! Feel the music."

And the tight muscles in their stomachs rubbed against one another as they glided around the small space to the music. They navigated the office floor the way seafarers sailed their boats. Their eyes locked in an embrace, and that entanglement was juicy and inviting.

Whirling around to the sounds of strings and their own heartbeats, the couple found a comfortable being of self. They were separate yet inseparable. If only the world could see them. Uptown Arlington folks would observe and say, "The raw attraction between man and woman is running high in the room." Downtown folks would say, *"It's a magnetism thang going on up in here, up in here."*

The music stopped.

Yet they continued to dance. Why? Because they weren't just dancing to music, they were dancing to dreams. Hopson thought of what he had been missing, being so engrossed in his work . . . someone to share his thoughts with, his love for music, his corny jokes, and his grumpiness about family pressure, his hopes and goals.

Imani thought of the strength she missed feeling when in the midst of a man's firm touch, someone to hold her and tell her everything would be all right . . . someone to laugh with and whisper sweet nothings and her heart's dreams to.

And then Hopson realized that there was no sound in the room. Just them moving. And he panicked. *No—I can't be falling in love with her. I can't. That'll ruin everything. I can't.*

Hopson released himself from their embrace and turned away. "You go back to the house. I've, uh, I've got more work to do."

"Are you sure?" Imani didn't want to leave the room.

"Yes, yes." Hopson fished around in his pants pocket. "Here's the key. Good night."

Imani took the keys, clutched them in her hand, mumbled "Good night, Hops," and left before he could say another word.

"C'mon, dog. What's the deal? Have you *even* talked to Imani?"

Taz ignored Biggie's question. Instead he cranked up the chatter about the upcoming event. "This concert is gonna be off the chain. Did you check out the lights we got rigged up?"

"Yeah-yeah. I saw 'em. But have you talked to Imani?"

"And look over here." Taz whipped by him. "We've got these funky glasses for people buying the expensive drinks. Slamming, huh?"

"Yeah, that's good but uh—"

"And we got the tickets printed!" Taz rushed towards a bar stool that had his jacket hanging on it. "They look good."

The phone rang. Taz whipped towards it. Biggie grabbed him by the shirt and yanked him in close. "Let it ring. And stop flying around here like a mosquito on crack. What did I just ask you?"

"I don't know."

"Oh you don't?" Biggie's eyes narrowed with anger. "I think I asked when was the last time I had to kick your ass, was it 1993 or today? I forget."

"Okay, man. Just chill. The answer is *no.*"

"Damn, Taz. What's your problem, dog?"

"It ain't my fault, Biggie. I've been trying but she won't answer my calls. But I know she's heard about the concert. Imani won't let me down."

"Let you down? C'mon, Taz. She's mad as hell at you, Maceo, and me too. We gotta make sure she's down with the program, you feeling me?"

"Yeah. Now gimme a break. Turn loose my shirt."

Biggie released him. "Sorry."

"You so jumpy, man."

"I should be. Mr. Watson is in real deep now. And who got him in? Me. Un-huh, yeah, me—because I'm trying to back you up. Now all this is riding on my rep. So there's no room for error, Taz. Everythang's gotta play and play right."

"But how are we gonna make sure Imani will do the concert?"

"That professor Negro is the one jamming us up."

"Yeah, Biggie . . . Hopscotch or Hucklebuck, whatever his name is. I saw a picture of him in some music journal Imani showed me. His punk ass is telling her she's the next jazz diva instead of the runaway rap star she's supposed to be."

"That's it! I don't know why we didn't think of it before, Taz."

"Think of what?"

"Instead of trying to force Imani to do something she may

not want to because she's pissed off, we'll get that professor guy to make sure she shows. Let the professor do the work for us."

"How are we gonna find him, Biggie?"

"Niggah, please. That campus ain't but yay big. Plus, I know they got a special parking lot for professors and administrators. I popped more than one or two cars outta there for a joyride in my day. He's gotta come out of that music building sometime."

"Okay, Biggie. Let's say we find him. Then what?"

"Then we get Godfather on him." Biggie opened his jacket revealing a gun in his waistband. "We make him an offer he can't refuse."

Chapter Twenty-one

Hopson had refused to see it. He really had. Sometimes we know things but we block them out of our thoughts, out of our heads. More often than not it's because we're afraid that what we do know calls for action and we're not ready to deal with it—*not at all*.

It hit Hopson right there in the office, there as he stood waiting for the music to begin, for their dance to start. Teasingly, time had spent itself slowly, and during that wait, that's when it hit him.

He was falling in love with Imani.

Where had the fall begun? he wondered.

Was it during the hours they spent together planning the music for the ball? Was it because during those times her eyes flashed like atmospheric energy? Or was it because of the hushed flutter that Imani's breathing made while studying a difficult chord change? Or how, when the disjointed lyrics finally became a clear-cut sound in her head, a soft phrase of understanding would leave her lips in the form of a sexy sigh, *Ummmm-huh . . . I see.*

But why hadn't Hopson seen this earlier?

Imani was beautiful. This he saw. His eyes relished the copper tone of her skin, the way she tilted her head, the way her nose flared with unchecked laughter, laughter whose high notes resembled sleigh bells as it rang around the room.

What else had Hopson seen?

He saw the way her eyes radiated during their dance. The music framed her face in time. He saw full lips the color of sun-soaked peaches pursed together, holding back the desire to ripen against his own.

That's what Hopson had seen. Now, what did he *feel?*

He felt fear. A crazy kind of fear that rumbled in the bottom of his stomach and rattled like marbled doubt in his head. This was not in his plan. His plan was clear-cut and sure. He was going to change Imani into a sophisticated jazz singer, win the bet, get his paper submitted, win the grant, ride the wave of publicity to its height, then leave Arlington for the Ivy League.

Where? Where did it say anywhere in the plan about falling in love? Nowhere. Fate was trying to pencil a whim into his plan. That was the crazy fear. Maybe he could deal with it, maybe . . . *if that had been the only thing.* Hopson imagined himself a strong person, mentally and emotionally. But the other fear he felt is what actually froze him.

It was the fear of love failing. There is nothing as painful as love blossoming—the excitement the heart feels in love, the anticipation of how that love will grow—and how quickly then failing. A slow failure of the heart can leave a trail of hurt as tangible as footprints in sand. Only a wave of pure emotion can possibly wash them away forever.

Hopson had been in love with his ex-girlfriend Serena but feared to voice it, to take charge, to be the type of man to grab his woman by the spirit and jump for joy. He had been the cautious type. Careful. Afraid to take a chance on love, afraid to put in the work, fearing that he would, like generations before him, get sidetracked and the family legacy would once again be deferred.

Hopson, like so many people before him, and the many who

would come after him, didn't know what to do. So with his mind boggled with thought, Hopson headed home, making sure it would be late and Imani would likely be asleep.

He exited the rear of the building and decided to cut through the parking lot to get his car and go home.

"That's him, Biggie." Taz pointed. "That's him right there."

Hopson didn't even see the two men coming.

They cut him off beneath one of the lampposts, near a corner.

Hopson looked from one man to the other. He slowly opened his jacket pocket. "Go ahead. Take my wallet and go."

Biggie laughed at him. "We not here to rob, man." He held out his hands. "These are fourteen-carat-gold chains on my wrists." Then he closed his fists. "We're here to straighten out a problem."

Hopson looked confused.

"I'm Biggie. This is my man, Taz."

"You're Taz?"

"Yeah, that's right."

"You used to be Imani's boyfriend."

"Whatcha mean 'used to be'?" Taz pushed Hopson up against the side of the building.

Biggie pulled him off. "Relax, dog. Reason first, violence second." Biggie spoke to Hopson. "He's been kindah feisty lately."

"Maybe because his girlfriend left him."

Taz lunged. Biggie caught him. "Whoa. Hey, Professor, you act like you wanna get your teeth knocked out or something."

"We're not here because of what I want. We're here because there's something *you* want."

Biggie turned to Taz. "See? Brah man knows how to cooperate." Then he smiled broadly at Professor Hopson. "We want you to make sure Imani shows up to perform at the grand opening of her daddy's club."

"She didn't say anything to me about performing."

"I'm telling you." Taz handed Biggie a flyer. He held it up in Hopson's face too close for him to actually read it. "See? Hot off the presses. Here's all the info. You make sure Imani is there and ready to go."

Biggie stuffed it in Hopson's breast pocket.

"What if I can't?"

Biggie straightened up, no longer amused. He showed Hopson the gun in his waistband. "I'll hurt you bad. Matter of fact, maybe I should give you a taste now. A little pistol-whipping can go a long way towards motivating a Negro."

"That's what I'm talking about," Taz growled.

Hopson cringed.

"Hey!" someone shouted.

All the men turned around.

It was Professor Sherman walking towards them. "What's going on back here?"

Biggie stared at Professor Sherman and he stared back.

Taz barked, his pride still hurt, "You handle him and I'll take care of Professor Big and Bad."

"Cool it, player," Biggie said, sizing up Professor Sherman. "We done here. Let's roll."

"Why, Biggie?"

"Get in the car." Biggie pushed Taz away. Then he turned to Professor Hopson. "And you remember what I said."

Biggie began backing away. He winked at the two men then disappeared into the night.

Hopson let out a sigh of relief.

Professor Sherman tried to comfort him. "You okay? What was that about?"

Hopson pushed him away. "Leave me alone."

"Wait a minute—"

"Ahhh!" Hopson brushed past Sherman. "Just leave me alone."

*   *   *

Sometimes when we are alone, we are able to ask ourselves questions that would be too jarring to speak of, or even too puzzling to think about, in the company of others. So in the space of a solo self, Imani asked, *Why? Why do I love Hops?*

She envisioned the way he held doors open for her and the way his eyes twinkled when he told her she was pretty. Imani imagined again his touch when they waltzed. The way his hand held her back, firm yet soft. It was the way he concentrated with his eyes closed, mouthing the sounds of a song before playing them aloud on the horn. It was the way he cared so much about making her a better performer. He drove her with passion. How could someone who had known her for such a short period of time do so much for her unless he loved her too?

But why then, Imani wondered, was he so unwilling to say it, to physically act on it?

Hops gave me the keys, she thought now, *and sent me home.*

Normally if Imani left before he did, she didn't wait up. He had a habit sometimes of staying until the early morning hours, then coming back just in time to shower and change for class.

Tonight, Imani decided to wait up for him.

I got something for you, Hops. Imani went to her things and found her sexiest piece of lingerie. *I'll be a lady at the ball for you, but I'm going to be a hottie in the bedroom tonight.*

When Hopson opened the door, the first thing he saw was a set of small candles lining a path from the door to Imani's bedroom. The scented wax smelled like roasting cherries.

Instinctively he walked that path to Imani's door, which was closed, and he knocked without hesitation. She opened the door and stuck her head out. Imani's hair was pinned up away from her face, exposing her neck and accenting the glow of her skin and the sparkle in her eyes. Hopson whispered the first words spoken between them.

"I need to talk to you."

"I'm through talking," she answered and pulled him into the bedroom.

By the candlelight there, Hopson saw that she had on a sheer violet wraparound. He had only seen that color once in his life-time, as a teenager, on a trip to Egypt with his family. Hopson had glanced down into the bottom of an ancient brook near a special prayer area that was more than one thousand years old. The sun penetrated the shallow water and went all the way to the bottom, striking a series of red pebbles. On fire, they turned violet.

Imani stood before him now on fire, wrapped from head to toe in violet.

She saw the worried look on his face and kissed him until it left. Imani put his arms around her waist and showed him how she liked to be held. She rested her chin against his chest and lis-tened to his escalating heartbeat as it tried to keep up with her racing thoughts of passion.

What they were together at that moment was love's essence personified. There were no downtown player hater ploys or up-town siddity cat-and-mouse games. They were the essence of what is good between a man and a woman. When one person cares for the other, what happens to them and their dreams?

The essence of love can't be penetrated because it's too deep. It can't sink because it's too heavy. It can only be absorbed when the elements are in order: when what is desired can be met equally. Ain't no lopsided ventures going on, period.

Here this man and woman cracked themselves open. Resis-tance became shell fragments and dropped to the floor. They hit silently like the clothes that were now falling off Hopson's back. The sheer fabric of her lingerie tingled against his skin. His thoughts of desire danced with her sensuality.

They opened themselves up to each other and shortcomings became long-ended pleasures. Each spent a thought on saving a little *something-something* for the next time melted away behind the electricity of wanting the night to last forever. But it did end with all their invisible phantoms caught and caged by what they had shared so lovingly together.

Hopson rose first thing in the morning. The soft breathing of the beauty sleeping next to him had been a comforting lullaby all night long. He smiled down at her. Hopson wanted nothing but the best for this woman who had given herself so freely and so emotionally. The trust Imani showed him with her talent and her heart overwhelmed him. Hopson reached down and let his fingertips barely graze the soft hairs curling at the base of her neck. He didn't want to wake Imani, just touch her. He walked past his clothes on the floor and picked up his jacket. The flyer stuck out like a jagged thorn and pricked his conscience.

Hopson grabbed the flyer and read it. He then looked over at Imani sleeping as sweetly as angels surely must fly. Hopson then heard the threats of Biggie in his head. He closed his eyes, made a decision, crushed the paper in his hand, showered, dressed, and left for a meeting with Chairman Perkins.

Shortly thereafter, Imani awoke. Her satisfaction filled ragged gaps that had been emotional potholes beneath her skin. She felt good to have loved the man she called Hops and to have felt his body, seamless against her own, flowing in the same direction as hers, the way streams merge into rivers.

The possibilities of unbridled love ran wild in her head, and the universe of what we desire opened up and became the road down which those possibilities traveled.

She thought of how their relationship would now progress, the high hopes she had for it. These were her thoughts as she headed to Shari's house to meet Rita, the dressmaker. Imani wanted to meet her there to make alterations on the gown she wanted for the ball. Imani and Shari both were really pleased at how the dress was turning out. Shari raved, "This dress is gonna be slamming, girl. I ain't lying. But come on now, Imani. I mean, don't you think it's a little too fancy for Club Maceo?"

"What?"

"I know it's being remodeled and all, plus it's the big grand opening too, but it might be a little much."

"This is *not* for Club Maceo. It's for the ball." Imani was matter-of-fact and watched as Rita stitched a loose seam at the tail of her gown. Ignorance can be a heavy door. Today Shari had to be the one to open it for Imani and show her the conflict that lay behind it.

"Imani, you *do know* the ball and the grand opening are on the same night. How you plan on being two places at once? You're bad, girl, but not *that* bad."

Imani didn't know. She'd run into a couple of friends who asked her about the concert, but blew them off, not wanting to hear the details. She'd thought, *Taz sure has a lot of damn nerve planning my life for me without asking. I'm not doing it.*

"You didn't know? Aww, damn, girl. I'm sorry. Truly sorry. I know how much this ball meant to you. But hey, keep your head up. Maybe the professor can swing it so you can perform there next year, huh?"

Imani swallowed hard. The saliva was like hot lava cruising down her throat. "I'm going to the ball."

"What? You're not gonna play Club Maceo?" Shari stayed Rita's hand and said, "Give us a few minutes, girl."

When the dressmaker left, Shari began grilling Imani. "How you gonna say no? The word is out about the concert. It's all over town. Taz and them are selling tickets like mad. They're telling everybody it's going to be off the hook and you're the headliner."

"I'm tired of Taz running my life. My daddy too. And throw Biggie in for good measure. They didn't ask me what I wanted to do, what I had planned, so hey, they deserve to get left hanging."

"Look, girl, I know you're mad at them for that fire thing—"

"Arson, baby, arson. Call it what it is, Shari."

"Okay fine. Arson. It was stupid. It was wrong. Haven't you ever done the wrong thing for the right reason?"

Imani shook her head.

"So you're gonna be low-down about this?"

"I'm going to the ball. I'm doing this for Hops. We've worked too hard—"

"Hops ain't your blood, Imani. I let it pass that you started talking proper. Fine. I let it pass that you stopped coming by the salon. I let it pass that you started staying uptown. But now you're straight tripping."

"I am not!"

"You are. Imani, you can't put that uptown man above your downtown family. What's up with that?"

"He's important to me. *This* is important to me."

"Awwww shit." Shari rocked back on her pumps. "You done fell in love with the man. Didn't I tell you not to fall in love with the man?"

"So what if I did?" Imani blurted out. "Why wouldn't I?"

"Because y'all don't belong together. You're from two different worlds. Speak two different languages, that's why."

"Shari, Hops has done everything he can to make things better for me. He took me in, groomed me, and showed me wonderful things. He cares about me not just because it's good for him. Not like Taz. Taz wants me to do this concert to make him look good. He doesn't want it for me."

"And that professor dude don't wanna prance you around like his trained pet in front of all those uptown mucky-mucks? That's not making him look good? Where's your common sense?"

"He's not like that, Shari."

"Please, if the man was *all that* he'd ah told you to help your family and do the concert."

"Hops doesn't even know about the concert. If he did, he would have told me and let me make my own decision. Hops respects me."

"News flash, homegirl. The professor knows about the concert."

"He doesn't!"

"Lies! Taz and Biggie told him. They even gave him a flyer and told him to make sure you were there. How's that for respect, huh? He didn't tell you because he wanted you to go to the ball. So what's the difference between him and Taz, huh?"

The words stung Imani to the core. She stepped out of the dress and began throwing on her clothes.

"Wait, Imani."

She blew past Shari and headed for Arlington to find Hopson. All the while she prayed, *Don't let it be true. Don't let it be true.*

Chapter Twenty-two

Truth can be as hard as a brick wall or as fragile as a bubble or as multisided as an octagon or as slanted as a triangle. Imani's search for the truth led her back to the campus. She stalked across the yard, eyes focused ahead, questions gyrating inside her brain. *Is Hops using me? Does he really love me? Did he know about the concert?*

Imani didn't see the security guard come up behind her, but she certainly felt his hand when he yanked her arm. "Where do you think you're going, Miss High and Mighty?"

"To the music department, if it's any of your business."

"To work?" the security guard sneered. He hated Imani ever since she got him in trouble with Chairman Perkins that day on the yard. He'd been waiting for a chance to get even.

"Yes, to work. Now move." Then as a sarcastic afterthought of politeness she added, *"Please."*

"You don't work here."

"I do too! I work for Professor Hopson!"

"Today's payday. You got a check?"

"I haven't been in yet. Besides, he cashes it for me."

"Yeah right. I did some investigating. You're not listed as an

employee and human resources never even heard of you. He's giving you money all right, *but uh, what for?*"

Imani hauled off and slapped the taste out of his mouth.

The security guard grabbed her and swung his hand back to slap Imani back.

"You better not!" Professor Sherman yelled. "Let her go."

The security guard slowly lowered his hand. "Professor Sherman. How long have you been standing there? Did you see? She hit me first. And she's been on campus, lying, saying that she works here."

"Imani *does* work here."

"But I checked with the employment office, Professor Sherman . . ."

"That's the music department's fault. We forgot to do the paperwork. She works here."

"How can that be?"

"Damn, man. Back up! Go punch a clock or break up a food fight in the cafeteria."

The security guard's face flushed with embarrassment. He released Imani and quickly left. Professor Sherman shot him in the back with stares before changing ammo and glancing sympathetically at Imani.

"You okay?"

Imani nodded. "I'm surprised you helped me."

"Why is that? I know I'm not as proper as your boy Hopson, but I'm still a gentleman."

"The guard is right, isn't he? I don't really work here. *Not officially.*"

"You didn't need him to figure that out, did you? If you really thought about it, you would have figured that out for yourself. But you didn't want to."

"But I've been helping Hops with his research . . ."

"So you *do* work here; officially or not—work is work. But

why explain it to me and anybody else around this joint? Hold your head up, girl."

"You talk funny for a professor."

"Yeah. That's because I didn't grow up like most of the faculty around here. I didn't have a lot of money. I went to a two-year college, then state school, and finally worked on my PhD at night to get here. My mama pushed me, and I made it."

"So you're like me, trying to fit in."

"No, I'm not, Imani. I'm not trying to change for anyone. I'm not trying to figure out who I am. So I'm not like you."

She cast her eyes down then looked up defiantly. "Sometimes change is good. It is, if it helps you accomplish something."

"Like what?" Professor Sherman challenged her. "Break it down. Be real for a minute."

"How can I get it out? Make you see? It's like I just get so tired sometimes. Tired of having to struggle to be noticed, to be heard. I get tired of trying to prove that I can be somebody, that I have skills. I just wanna show the whole world. I wanna say, *Nah-nah, see there? Look at me. Look what I bring to the table and guess what, now the table is full.*"

Professor Sherman laughed. "You remind me of somebody. Somebody special."

"Who? Some ex-girlfriend you played on?"

Professor Sherman screeched like a frightened cat and clawed the air. "Baby got back *and* claws, huh?"

Imani laughed. When she stopped laughing Professor Sherman answered her question.

"No, Imani, you don't remind me of an ex-girlfriend. You remind me of my mother. You're a downtown girl with a lot of heart."

"Thanks. And speaking of heart, I'm about to flex some right now. I need to find Hops. I've got to straighten some things out. Have you seen him?"

"Maybe."

"Please?"

"Okay, follow me," Professor Sherman said. "I know where he is."

But little did they know that they were headed to a room that was peppered with conflicting ideas and colliding egos.

Chairman Perkins was standing up, angrily thumping the table with his fist. "I'm just two seconds away from tossing you *lock, stock, and black butt* off this campus."

"What for?"

"What for?" Chairman Perkins glanced up to the heavens. "What for, he asks?"

"Yes, what for?"

"Because it's all over campus that you and Imani are living together. Do you realize how that looks? And in the house that's reserved specifically for Arlington Fellows?"

"What was I supposed to do, Chairman? She had some trouble at home. She came in the middle of the night, with no money and nowhere else to go. She was running from a doggish boyfriend."

"What about after that? You could have found her somewhere else to stay. Did you try?"

"Look, Chairman. It wasn't that cut and dry. Imani is important to me. I couldn't just boot her off to just any old place."

"What are you trying to tell me, Professor?"

"I'm trying to tell you that I care about Imani as a person, as a woman, as a phenomenal talent. That's what I'm trying to tell you."

"I'm sorry that I ever made that silly bet." Chairman Perkins paced back and forth. "I pushed you into it. I don't know what made me think that you'd be able to turn a ghetto girl into a jazz diva. We'll let the jazz band play at the ball. The bet is off."

"Don't call it off! I can win. Give me a chance."

"So that's it," Imani whispered.

She and Professor Sherman were standing in the doorway of the faculty lounge. Her voice grew louder, more surprised.

"I was a bet?"

"Imani," Hopson sighed. "Wait a minute. It's not how it sounds, not how it looks."

"What was the bet? Huh, Hops? What would you win if you got your little plaything to do tricks for the uptown folks at the ball?"

"Imani . . ."

"Young lady . . ."

"Don't you mean 'ghetto girl,' Chairman?" She asked Hopson again, "What would you win? Tell me!"

"Chairman Perkins would enter my paper in the grant competition instead of Professor Sherman's."

"That's it? Why so cheap, Hops? You shouldah put a couple of bills down too, dammit. You could've really pimped me then, *player-player.*"

"Imani, don't talk like that."

"Like what? Like a downtown girl? *I am a downtown girl.* And till now, some kindah scary way, I forgot that. But don't you have sense enough to know that you can't make something out of nothing? You're not Frankenstein. I'm no monster. I had this diva in me all the time. It was just waiting to get out. You're no miracle worker, Hops."

"Imani, it wasn't like that. I mean it was, at first, just a bet, but after a while—"

"Hush," Imani said very low. "Hush-hush."

Hopson got up and reached for her.

"Hush," she said once more, the word gurgling in her throat. Imani walked over to Hopson and kissed him softly. "Bye."

And then she left.

Hopson stood there with his heart in chaos and his mind confused about what in the world he should do next.

                    *   *   *

Chaos was about to break out in Taz's little studio. It was packed with people. They were FuBu, Phat Farm, Sean John, Nike, and Adidas down. It was a listening party of sorts. Taz had several music tracks he had put together ready to go. Some of the rappers had asked their friends to come by and check it out.

Somebody brought the wine.

Somebody else brought a couple of buckets of chicken.

Nobody knew who fired the shots. The first bullet tore through the window, just missing a kid turning around his woman to grind up against the wall on a slow jam.

The next shot blasted a lamp, sending sharp pieces of plastic flying through the air.

The third bullet hit the sofa; a sofa already propped up against the wall, wounded from years of abuse.

The last bullet shattered the top windowpane, ripped the paper shade to tinsel, ricocheted off a set of metal burglar bars and struck . . . Biggie. He clutched his upper body. Blood began oozing through his fingers before he fell to the floor unconscious, still as stone.

The stillness that gripped Biggie was the polar opposite of what Imani was experiencing at that exact same moment. Everything about her . . . and everything around her . . . was in a state of constant movement. Her mind roamed the scenes of her life. Imani's heart raced inside her chest. The wind swirled the braids on her head as she walked outside. Her feet felt bloated on the ends of her ankles. Each step was as heavy as the thoughts that teetered back and forth across her heart. Imani wasn't exactly sure where her support was coming from right at that moment.

Could it be from the hurt that she was feeling? Nothing is quite as miserable as a love pain. The ache usually starts slow, growing in size and intensity like a special effect in some high-tech horror film. A bulge in the gut, it bloats and hardens like concrete that somehow keeps a person from experiencing sorrow's meltdown. Question is, is that the best thing?

Like the rappers ask, what's mo' better? Would it be mo' better to just collapse all at once shedding torment's cocoon? Or is Imani's current plight mo' better—just keeping on with the keeping on, while still aching?

Imani had her notebook with her. The fire at Club Maceo had somehow ignited a creative burn in her. Imani had been cramming her new notebook with both rhymes and lyrics now that she had unearthed her phenomenal voice.

They were songs for her people: for the little lady who stood on the corner by the drugstore, selling half her painkillers so she could get grocery money for her grandbabies. Imani wrote lines for the teenage boy down the block who had mad skills, not with a basketball on the hard court, but with a Bunsen burner in the school lab, a science scholarship waiting despite parents who never helped with homework because they didn't believe in him or his dream.

Movement swirled all around Imani as she walked. Before she realized it, she was standing in a crowd at the Greyhound bus station, listening as one of the neighborhood rappers threw down. A litany about bitches and hos rolled off his tongue and like shrapnel tore into the women standing around evaluating his flow. Double-breasted in the armor of "heard that before," they were unfazed and unmoved. They didn't cheer or blink, merely stood like statues and thought, *Come on with it.*

Slinking away to weak applause and the clink of small silver coins being sorrowfully slung into a cap, the rapper who would be king left a pauper, robbed of his confidence.

Someone in the crowd of hip-hop subjects recognized the queen. "Imani, that you, girl? Where you been, huh? Where you been?"

Imani's mind went blank as she searched for an answer.

Where had she been? Figuratively, she'd been in a wonderland of sorts, a place so different from where she had grown up. She'd been in a place mingling with the new talented tenth, the young black folks that had sprung up from the dust of Dubois, from the zenith of Zora, from the essence of Ellington and the spiritual bosom of Booker T.

Imani had experienced a musical growth spurt with the help of tender care by her man Hops. But she had been more than just a snatcher, a grabber, and a creative jacker who took someone else's stuff and then played it off like it was her very own. Imani gave back. She helped Hops too.

As Imani walked now, she heard herself asking the question, the question she had asked one day several weeks ago, when a student came and asked for help and Hops had turned him away.

"What's up with that, Hops?"

"Excuse me?" he had asked. They were in his office.

"I've never been to college but I know that a teacher is supposed to help the students whenever they ask. Why don't you keep office hours like the other professors?"

"I stay after class and answer questions then." Hopson felt flush around the collar. "Now, where were we?"

"After class? What's that? Ten minutes or so. Can't be any more than that. You get to the office too quick."

"So where's the memo, Imani? You're the new department chairman now or what?"

"Don't trip—"

"Can't you find another word for trip?"

"Mad. Pissed off. How's that, Hops?"

"*Keep coming, lady,*" he said sarcastically. *Why am I defending myself?* he thought.

"Defensive?"

He blinked.

"You give in class. I understand that. I feel you, Hops. You're laying out your knowledge for them. You do it for me, too, sometimes. You lay it out so we can pick it up and grow ourselves. But sometimes, Hops, you've gotta feed it to people. You have to prepare it and present it with joy, then feed it. People don't always have the strength to do for themselves; they need to be fed. Am I making sense?"

More than Imani could ever appreciate, she had hit on the head what Hopson had missed for quite a while. Why wasn't he having more fun teaching at Arlington? Was the burden of success smothering the way he passed on the legacy of love for music?

"You're trying so hard that you're blocking your students out. Open up a little, Hops. It don't hurt. It don't cost nothing."

And slowly Hopson had begun to have fun with the students. Imani sat in on a class or two, watching. One time, the band made a mistake while practicing a serious jazz piece. Hops didn't scowl or fuss. Instead he broke out in a spontaneous rendition of "Pop Goes the Weasel." They all laughed. Hops made fun of the honest mistake. He became easier and the band began to open up to him the way flowers open up to the sun.

"Hey, Imani, where you been?"

A little girl named Tonya asked the question; a little girl with thick cornrows, big, pretty eyes, and love missing at home. She and her girlfriend liked to hang out by the bus station and listen to the performers. Imani would play to her sometimes. Tonya loved it. She asked the question again.

"Hey, Imani, where you been?"

Imani snapped out of her trance. She answered, "Far away, it feels like."

One of the other rappers shouted, "Well bust off a rap for us, girl. You've been missed!"

Hands pushed Imani forward and she stepped into the center of the crowd, stood on the bench, and looked at the eager, smiling faces waiting to be fed.

Imani, fearing to disappoint, reached inside herself for one of her old standards, one of her can't-miss wordsmith masterpieces. She pulled it up but couldn't play it right.

Those are the words, she thought as she said them. *That is the beat,* she thought as she kept tempo with a bob and weave.

When Imani finished the bus station crowd cheered out of respect for performances past. Little Tonya and her friends cheered the loudest, not wanting Imani to feel bad. But she did.

Someone whispered as she walked by, "Wherever she was, she lost her edge."

Suddenly a car pulled up, screeching to a halt. Slowly the window began to roll down. Everyone turned. One of the neighborhood rappers stuck his head out and shouted, "Did y'all hear? Somebody done busted off some shots in Taz's studio."

Imani jerked around. "What?"

"Yeah, Imani . . . some folks got hit. Biggie, for sure. They all over at county hospital."

"Take me there. Quick."

Chapter Twenty-three

When Imani got to the hospital, everyone was praying. She noticed that even the hardcore rappers had their heads down, trying to play it off. Their lips hardly moved. Their eyes were barely closed. But they were praying. Each breath they exhaled was a blast of hope, shot into the universe like penicillin to fight off the fear that was plaguing the air.

How bad? Imani thought. *And how many?* "Biggie for sure," she had heard. For sure . . . *Biggie.*

She recalled when Biggie was the neighborhood protector, using his fearlessness and strength for the weak ones like her and Taz.

Life had hardened that courage and hung it around his neck like a shiny thug-life badge. He wore it proud, although Imani could see that it was wearing him down and making him a target too.

God, she thought, *let Biggie and Taz be okay. Please God.* Her thoughts were abundantly decent and a little bit selfish. *We've been mad at each other for so long now. If I lose Biggie or Taz now, I'll never forgive myself.*

At the hospital, Imani spotted Shari and Ma June huddled in a corner, holding each other, crying. The words darted off her lips. "Is Biggie gonna be okay?"

"It's bad, sweet Jesus," Ma June whispered. "He's in surgery."

"How about Taz?" Imani blurted out, unable to hold back her fear any longer. "How's Taz?"

"He's fine," Shari managed to say. "Not a scratch."

Tears of relief ran down Imani's face.

"Just Biggie got hit bad. Two other girls had flesh wounds, they're bandaged up and gone already."

Imani was barely listening, looking around for Taz.

She spotted him through a set of double doors, helping one of the wounded girls into a van that had pulled up to the emergency room entrance. Imani ran to him. Taz turned and rushed towards her.

"I was so scared for you," she said, hugging him.

"Don't tell nobody, but I was scared for me too."

"What happened?"

"That's what we want to know," two police officers said, stepping up. "You're Taz, right?"

He grunted and gave them a jerky head bob.

"You own that jackleg studio where the shooting took place?"

Another jerky head bob.

"You got a mouth; use it," one of the officers growled.

Taz scowled and said nothing.

One of the cops grabbed him by the front of his clothes and jerked him nose to nose.

"Taz didn't do anything!" Imani shouted.

Everyone in the emergency room was watching now. Still the police officer didn't loosen his grip. "Well if he's a victim, he'd better start acting like one. We're trying to get this paperwork done. To tell the truth I don't give a damn who shot up the place. Half the punks in there must have had it coming. I'm just trying to get my last statement and go home."

"Taz, please. Just tell him whatever it is he wants to know."

"All right." Taz slowly pulled back. "All right, let's go."

Taz and the cops went over to a corner and began talking. After about twenty minutes, a white-haired doctor came out of the emergency room. Imani rushed over to be with Shari and her mother. The doctor broke the news.

"He'll make it. That's a tough son of gun."

All Biggie's boys laughed and slapped five. Ma June sobbed. Biggie would be in intensive care, just two doors down from the mailman.

Shari turned to the cops who were now finished questioning Taz. "Y'all should be out looking for whoever shot my brother."

"Honey," one of the cops said, "your brother is a strong-arm man. The list of suspects is longer than the welfare line on the first of the month. Just be thankful he's alive and nobody got killed."

"That's it?" Taz barked. "Y'all ain't gonna try and find out who did it?"

The cops shrugged halfheartedly and walked away.

"If they won't, I will." Mr. Watson took off his hat. He had been quietly standing off to the side. "Put the word out on the street, everybody. I want the name of the shooter, and no price is too high."

All these years, Imani's dream of performing at the ball had sat high on a shelf inside her. By her own hand, Imani sent that dream tumbling down. There in the hospital she made up with Shari and Taz, and later her father, who came to pick her up. She promised them all that she would perform at the grand opening of Club Maceo on May 8.

Imani went back to Hopson's house to pack her things. Fate was merciful and he was not there. The space itself was intimidating enough.

When we leave a place where we have grown and where we have loved, it's difficult. Rooms with walls and beams suddenly become memories with sights and sounds. Imani picked up her music notebook on the table by the fireplace and got a whiff of the smoky wood that reminded her of the many nights they had sat there, flames flickering.

Hopson sat on the floor at her feet, she in the oversized chair behind him. They traded notes. He'd play a note on the horn; she'd match it with her voice. He'd get tricky and put treble in it. She'd challenge, "Oh, so you wanna take me there?" And then she'd match the sound in her own powerful register.

Imani heard their laughter now as she continued to collect things. She felt the soft plop on her back when they had their pillow fight over who was right about a chord change. Imani had socked it to the brother, making him lose his breath and his balance. "Who knew," Hops had said, looking up from the floor, "that you were that strong?"

Imani knew. She felt that she was growing in this relationship. Although it was teacher and student, man to woman, it was really, deep down to the nitty gritty, person to person. What we can see in others is often a blind spot for them.

Imani saw the pressure that this young man she nicknamed Hops had put himself under.

"Why are you so hard on yourself?" she'd asked him one day while taking a walk by the water. It was a beautiful day with a soft breeze blowing.

"I don't know that I'm so hard on myself. Driven maybe."

"If you could have a wish right now, what would it be?"

"C'mon, Imani, that's kid stuff."

"Did you grow up? I didn't and truly don't want to. Not when it comes to wishes. What would you wish, Hops?"

He spoke without thinking. "I'd wish for tenure and a department chairmanship."

Imani stopped walking.

"What?"

"You'd waste a wish on that? Focus is one thing, Hops. Being whacked is another."

"What would you wish for, Imani? Money? Fame?"

"I'd wish for love."

"All women do."

"And every man should. Hops, I'd wish that God would send somebody to love me right. I'd wish for a love that made me melt from the inside out."

Then Hopson reached down and grabbed a handful of violets. "Would you settle for some flowers from an admirer?"

"That's a start."

What Imani had made her mind up to do now was to start over after the concert. How could she explain that in the midst of this upheaval, and this cold relief of Biggie's survival, that she'd had what seemed like a revelation worth shouting about?

When we realize what is important to us, long after it's gone, our hearts shout out *why* after the loss. It's so weird sometimes to see someone special leaving your life. They *never ever* disappear in a poof, an evil trick being played out in life's spotlight. You see them leaving almost in slow motion beneath shadows. Inch by inch they vanish from your scene. They leave you thinking, *Could I have stopped it? What went wrong? Why does it hurt so badly?*

Imani vanished from Hopson's scene. He knew when he put the key in the door that she wouldn't be there when he opened it. Hopson stepped into a space that had been changed by another's scent, another's laughter, another's hopes and dreams living within the walls. And now, with those elements gone, the makeup of the space changed once again. But not back to the original state. Oh, no. Not hardly.

The original state for Hopson had something missing. Wasn't talent; old boy had plenty of that. Wasn't desire; that was pulsing full blast through his veins. What was it? It was someone to share his life with, the ups and the downs, the whatever days.

It was the body of a woman lying next to him at night. A

body with skin that was soft to the touch and yielding to his fancy. It was an open ear waiting to be filled, never tiring of hearing about his trials. A tongue wagging with the words "You can."

We are all insecure in one way or another, all vulnerable. Vulnerability is nothing but a gap in the spirit. Someone else can fill that gap, but only if you let them and only for as long as you let them.

Imani filled that gap for Hopson, because he let her for a fleeting moment, and that moment changed his life. He now had to think about things.

Hopson took a hot shower to soothe the muscles jittering nervously in his back and neck. After the shower, he built a fire and sat by it, robed in cotton and clothed in a weary mind.

Memories began to pester him: especially Imani's voice, the cream rising to the top of the scale. Her laugh, soft, falling away, so real yet so elusive . . .

He remembered it best from a visit to the playground. There happened to be one located halfway between the university and the downtown neighborhood where Imani grew up. It was neutral ground where both uptown kids and downtown children played together. Oddly enough, until age seven or so, they all played there together pretty well. But right about the third grade is when society's magnetic pull kicked in; *like began to stick with like;* the ways parted and the older kids began to amuse themselves closer to home in their less lovely but status quo playgrounds.

Imani had to drag Hopson there. He wanted to work a little longer and she had a burn to play. She wanted to say hi to Shari, who brought her little girl there on Monday afternoons when her shop was closed.

"Hops this is Shari. Shari, Professor Hopson."

"Nice to meet you, I've heard wonderful things about you," he said and lightly kissed Shari's hand.

"Ya don't say," Shari purred and cut her eyes at Imani. "I'm sure Imani's description of me hasn't done me a bit of justice."

Hops stifled a laugh. He saw quickly that Shari was beginning to put on airs.

"You're right. She wasn't even close in describing your beauty and your sophistication."

"Say that *once more*, Professor, but louder so the world will know." Shari laughed.

"I'm sure," Hopson said with a wink, "that wherever you go, all the world knows you're there."

"Mama," Baby called out, "catch!"

She had struggled to get to the top of the slide and was now waiting for someone to catch her down at the bottom.

"I got her, girl." Imani ran over, dodging kids who were on bikes and rolling around in the sandbox. "Beep! Beep! Coming through!"

The little girl smiled and whirled down the slide, finding comfort in Imani's waiting arms. "Together?" Imani suggested. Baby stuck her finger in her mouth and giggled a yes. The two ran around and made their way back up the slide. When Imani looked down, she saw Hops standing there.

"Come on. I gotcha."

"You can't catch us both."

"Where's your faith? You'll never touch the ground."

"No way!" Imani shouted playfully. "Move!"

Hopson looked surprised. He asked two little boys standing nearby. "Feel that!" he made a muscle. "Strong!" he growled.

"Strong!" they growled back.

"Strong-strong!" Hopson began chanting.

The boys grinned at him and began chanting with him. Soon the entire playground had joined in.

"Okay!" Imani laughed at the top of the slide. "Look out below, here we come."

And they came whirling down the slide, the wind pushing

them with abandon. Hopson bent his knees and caught them, their momentum knocking him onto his back.

"See?!" Imani said as she and the little girl practically sat on Hopson's chest.

"See what? I told you you wouldn't hit the ground."

And everyone watching began to laugh.

"Whoa." Imani began to tilt over. "Don't let me fall, Hops."

"Don't worry. I won't let you go."

"I won't let you go." That's what you said, Hopson thought to himself. *That was then, and this is now. Should I let her go? Can I let her go?*

Hopson laid back, closed his eyes, and asked God to speak to his heart with the answer.

Chapter Twenty-four

While Hopson was looking for answers, Maceo was asking Imani questions. He crept into her room, now partially remodeled, and sat on the edge of her bed. The curtains were pulled back and the moon was full and dead center in the window. Its rays shone on her face and he could see her eyes fluttering as she struggled to keep them closed, pretending to be asleep.

"When I was a young man courting your mother, I loved to steal quiet time. We would sit on the fire escape in New York on hot nights, after I'd played a late set. We'd get a bottle of wine and we'd catch a breeze and talk about our dreams. No matter what else went on during the day 'tween us or at the club, we'd be honest and open with each other out on that fire escape."

Imani abandoned her feigned attempt at sleep and turned over. She sat up and looked at her father, then placed her arm around his neck. Maceo gently kissed her wrist and patted her hand.

"People tried to warn your mother about me. 'Hotheaded,' they said. 'Spirited,' she'd argue. 'Talented but the cat's going nowhere,' they said. 'A star held back by jealous folk,' she'd argue. Even when I advised her not to sign a contract with that white producer and he went on and made another woman a star. 'Not my time,' she said. Even after the two albums I produced for her flopped. 'Be encouraged,' she said."

"Mama was supposed to stick by the man she loved. If she didn't who would?"

"The loyalty that she had? I see that in you, Imani. But . . ."

"But what, Daddy?"

Maceo patted her hand, kissed it. "But nothing. I just want the best for you. I want you to make it where me and your mother messed up."

"Is that worrying you?"

"Always, baby."

Imani let her head come to rest gently on Maceo's shoulder. "It's going to be okay, Daddy. You'll see. And you know what?"

"Hmmm?"

"I used to be unsure of a lot of things most of the time."

"Couldn't tell it, baby."

"Oh, I can fake the funk now. Yes I can."

Maceo laughed at his daughter.

"But now, Daddy, after everything, I realize something."

"What's that?"

"Something important about myself."

"What?"

Imani leaned forward and rested her chin on her father's shoulder. Her lips were near his ear as she told him the discovery she had made.

It was a discovery rather miraculous; not like the stars lining up with purpose in the sky to form a galaxy, or the sun chasing the moon around the globe, or even flowers budding beneath the dark ground to emerge full blown into the light.

Not miraculous like generations overcoming the aftereffects of slavery or the Holocaust; not miraculous like the conception of life or the sovereignty of birth.

Imani's discovery was miraculous in the way that we have

to struggle to learn real things about ourselves. Miraculous in the sense that many people live a lifetime and don't have a handle on why they do the things they do. They never learn what they want from loved ones or what their loved ones need from them.

It was miraculous that she had been able to reach down and look inside herself and decide what she needed to do for Imani. What was important to her and what she needed from those she loved.

That was one miracle.

Could there be room for two in one lifetime?

Would Imani have the courage to act on her discovery and would those who loved her love her enough to act on it too?

Sometimes we don't make decisions, we claim them from somebody else's lost and found.

All that had happened now forced Professor Hopson to take a good look at himself with skeptical eyes. He had to look. Examine. A man is not like a snake that can shed skin and change or like a turtle with a shell to hide in. Everything good and bad is for the seeing.

Hopson knew that he loved Imani and that she was a special woman. But he also realized that he had tried to shape her without regard to her natural flow. Imani had found his image and desires for her and claimed them as her own. Just as he had been making decisions trying to claim the lost dreams of his family legacy.

He went home thinking. His thoughts were flying around in his head. The more he thought, the more emotional he became. Hopson knew that Imani had grown and still had more growing to do. Could she do it with him around? Didn't Imani need space to think on her own? To flourish on her own?

And what about him? Could he be so near yet stay away to give her the ability to grow? To give Imani the space to make her own choices? Hopson knew that he loved Imani. And it was that love that made him *not* want to smother her. He wanted to give her space and time to decide what she needed. And he hoped to God that those needs would somehow include him. These were the primary thoughts that had been flying around in his head. They found the exit and became his solution.

Where would he go? He had the offers from the Big Ten and the Ivy League. Now they seemed so unimportant. He realized that they didn't really need him as much as the students here did. Maybe another small black college? Or maybe just take a year off and travel. Something different. Something to take his mind off of . . . *her*. Maybe he needed space too?

Hopson tried to reach Imani to talk to her. But it was no use. He got no answer at her home or on her cell number. She *refused* to return his calls.

Sometimes when people try to reach out to us when we're hurt, we can't reach back. The hurt is too fresh. The ache is still in the gut. Our mouth is still dry. Our eyes remain watery. Emotions constantly bubble at our core. They're forced down by us. We use pride as a cork, or even worse, anger.

Imani was hurt. She wouldn't answer her cell, erased the messages without listening.

Shari called her on it, in a way that only a best friend can. They were at Ma June's house, on the block where they grew up, sitting on the front steps like old times. Shari leaned back, crossed her legs, and fired off. "I gotta say it. Wouldn't be worth a dime if I didn't. What the hell are you doing, Imani?"

"Don't start nothing, Shari. I'm trying to cool out over here."

"So? I'm tired of watching you hurt. Plus you're making yourself hurt worse. Why don't you call the man back?"

"You don't even *like* him, Shari."

"I didn't say I didn't like him. You and Taz had a thing, a

thing that you wanted and it was flowing, but now I see different."

"How, Shari? How are you seeing different?"

"Old boy Hops is good for you."

Imani couldn't help but laugh. "Hold up, girl. *You* were the one ragging on me about changing up and getting siddity and all that."

"You *were.* Your silly ass went overboard."

"Thanks a lot."

"Imani, what he showed you was the talent you have inside. And you have a confidence that you didn't have before. He'll challenge you in a relationship; help you find all the aspects of you. These are things I'm not sure you would have started on your own. And not with Taz for damn sho'."

"I know. I've been around Taz lately and it's no good, Shari."

"You've outgrown him, girl. Simple as that."

"But so many people that he's loved have left him. I can't just roll, can I?"

"Pity is a poor-ass substitute for love, girl."

"I love him."

"Always will." Shari laughed. "That first piece of skins is a monster. You'll always cherish that."

Imani and Shari high-fived each other. Shari put her arm around Imani's shoulders. "But it's more than that. You know that, right?"

"I know . . . I love me and I see things and want to do things with music that I only dreamed of before. But not Taz's dream. Not Hops's either. My sound. My music. After the concert, that's what I'm focusing on . . . me. Me and my dreams."

"And which man do you love the most and which one won't turn your dreams into a nightmare? Huh, Imani? Answer that?"

Imani knew the answer. She blushed.

"G'on and call Hops back, girl. Y'all talk it out."

Imani hugged Shari and went to make the call. She knew Hops; he'd be in class now. She didn't want to bother him there. So Imani called his office and would leave a message telling him she wanted to talk.

His voice mail made Imani's mouth and her spirit drop.

"Hi. This is Professor Hopson. I am out of the office right now. At the end of the semester I will be leaving Arlington. If you are calling about the summer program, please contact Professor Rick Sherman . . ."

That's why he was calling. *He's leaving.* He was calling me to tell me good-bye. Imani felt her insides wring backward and forward like the center of a washing machine set on high. That was her answer. She loved him but he didn't love her, at least not enough to stay. Imani slowly hung up the phone. *He's leaving.* Tears welled up in Imani's eyes because for this new hurt, Imani was not prepared.

When things in our lives start changing, we think we can prepare for them. But God likes to do the planning and you *never know* what his moves will be.

That next morning Hopson went straight to his office. He began reorganizing, prioritizing things that needed to be done before he left. He planned on a smooth transition away from Arlington. No fuss. No muss. And the way that Chairman Perkins had been riding him, the old man was probably glad to see him go.

Professor Hopson looked at the offers that he had worked so hard to get from the Ivy League and the Big Ten. Hopson just shook his head. They were so unimportant now. He tossed them on top of the desk when Chairman Perkins suddenly barged in.

"Professor Hopson!"

"Chairman. Did you get my letter of resignation?"

"Yes I did. I was stunned. What's going on?"

"I just need to step down right now."

"Are you sick?"

"No."

"Is your family all right?"

"Yes, everybody's fine."

"Well what's the problem? Why resign? If you need a vacation, take one, but don't resign."

"I need to think some things through, Chairman. That's all."

Chairman Perkins walked over to the desk where Hopson was sitting. "I hate to see such a young, brilliant teacher walk away so abruptly. I've been hard on you, sure, but that's the old-school way of grooming talent."

"It's not that."

"Then what is it?" Chairman Perkins's face was wracked with concern. He leaned over. "Can I help?"

And when he leaned over, Chairman Perkins accidentally knocked over a pile of papers on the desk. He and Hopson both reached for them.

"Dartmouth?" Chairman Perkins read the letterhead of one of the job offers that Hopson had received. "Michigan too."

"Wait a minute."

"So you want to *think?* You want to get paid, you mean. The big universities with their fat salaries, their ivy walls, and their predominantly white student bodies are calling your name, huh?"

"No—that's not it. That's not why I'm leaving. And I doubt if I'll even take one of those offers."

"Dammit boy, don't take me for a fool. It's clear. You're selling out. Why not have the guts to say that?" Chairman Perkins crushed the letters in his fist. "We scuffle and we scrape here for new dorms and scholarships and salaries, yes. We fall short. But what we *are not* short on here at Arlington is *pride* and *tradition,* and if you can't value that above all else—"

"You're wrong. I swear that's not it."

"Then what is it, Professor?"

Hopson swallowed. "It's personal and none of your business, Chairman. I'm sorry."

"Consider your resignation accepted." Chairman Perkins knocked the rest of the papers off the desk. "Immediately."

Chapter Twenty-five

Sherman brushed past the moving men and barged into the house. His anger was churning as he glanced from box to box.

One of the moving men noticed him and joked, "A tux is kindah fancy for helping somebody move, ain't it, brah?"

Sherman shot him a deadly look.

"My bad."

"Where's Professor Hopson?"

"Upstairs packing up his stuff."

Sherman entered the room. He saw Hopson dressed in sweats with his back to the door, bent over and taping up a box. Sherman put his foot on Hopson's butt and shoved him down onto the floor.

Hopson rolled over. "What the hell is your problem?"

"You," Sherman answered, sitting on the edge of the bed looking down at him. "You. You're my problem. I just left the professors' reception at the ball. They say you quit."

"Sorry. You should have heard it from me first. But . . ."

"It's true?" Sherman sucked his teeth. "Why?"

"I don't want to go into it, Sherman. Please. Back off."

"Hopson, man, I tell you the truth. I figured you for a lot of things, man: a stuffed shirt, kindah uppity, but never a quitter. I never thought you'd quit."

"Who cares what you think?" Hopson rose from the floor. He threw an empty box at Sherman, who caught it. "Either shut up and load a box or get out."

Sherman tossed the box on the floor. "Not until I get my say."

"I don't want to hear it. I need to get out of here."

"What you *need* is Imani and she needs you. What about her, huh?"

"I don't get you, Sherman. I'm your main competition around here and now I'm finally out of your way. Why do you care if I leave or not? Or about anything else I do for that matter?"

" 'Cause I care about people. And as for our rivalry, so what? Yeah, I'm competitive. I'm tough. And I've made it where I am today because of those two things."

"I know that, Sherman. And I respect that."

"I'm proud of it, too, but that's not how I wanted it, man. I wish it hadn't been so damn hard. I always wanted somebody to help me coming up. I looked high and low for a mentor. I should-ah never had to struggle like I did, struggle so hard for so long."

"Look, Sherman. I don't have time for all this. Besides, I don't even know where you're trying to go with this. So just leave me alone, okay?"

"I can't. Wish to God that I could, but I can't. See, once I realized the grit that Imani had, plus the talent, I thought, Wow, here's somebody who can go places and she's hooking up with somebody who can help her get there. Imani will get what I never had early on. A break."

"Imani doesn't need my help. She's super talented. She'll be fine. I've made her mad and she needs time away from me. That's the best thing for her."

"She said that?"

Hopson shrugged.

Sherman put his foot on the box Hopson was trying to tape.

"No, Imani didn't say that. I just know that. Now, move your foot."

"If I put it somewhere else, you're not gonna like it."

Hopson squared his shoulders.

Sherman dared him. "Now you can try and move it for me. But I'd hate to mess up this tux I just rented. So why don't you just shut your ass up and listen?"

"Talk fast."

"Okay. There's going to be a surprise guest at the ball tonight. One of Arlington's most distinguished graduates. Guess who?"

"I don't want to guess, Sherman, all right?"

"Play the game. Guess who?"

"*Okay* . . . that senator from Carolina?"

"Not him. Lionel Whitmore."

"Lionel Whitmore?! He's one of the top music producers in the world. Everybody wants to work with him."

"And why not? He's got three Grammys of his own and three more producing other artists. I just read in the trades that he's about to launch his own record label."

Hopson wondered out loud. "He hasn't been to the ball in years. Why now?"

"Next year is his fortieth anniversary in the business. PBS is following him around doing a documentary. He wanted to give Arlington some exposure."

"That's great." Then Hopson gave his friend a puzzled look. "So why are you over here bugging me? You need to be at the ball trying to meet Whitmore."

"Somebody else needs to meet him more than you *or* me."

Hopson thought. "Imani! She needs to be there. This would be the opportunity of a lifetime for her."

Sherman put his foot on the floor. "Now you're feeling me."

Hopson began pacing. "But she's got that concert to perform for her father."

"Forget that. Imani needs to be at that ball. And you're the only one who can get her there."

"She won't listen to me."

Professor Sherman spoke passionately. "Yes she will."

"Are you sure?"

Sherman looked at him sarcastically. "Do you love her?"

"What?"

"Negro, I asked, do you love her?"

Emotion rushed the word out of Hopson's mouth. "Yes."

"Then what are you waiting on? Unpack your tux and go get her."

Hopson began ripping open one of the boxes at his feet. He stood up. "But I'm not sure where her father's club is. I gotta find that flyer." He started looking around. "It's called Club Maceo but I don't know where it is . . ."

"I know where it is. I'll drive you there."

The two men exchanged a long glance, then smiled at each other before shaking hands. Sherman said what Hopson knew in his heart.

"Hurry up, man. Opportunity wears a fast watch."

If opportunity wears a fast watch, fate is timeless. Hopson and Sherman pulled up to Club Maceo. There was a crowd of teenagers and young adults waiting outside to be let in. The crowd included rappers from the bus station as well as Tonya and her young girlfriends. The two professors cut right to the front of the line. A group of hip-hop she-devils weren't having it.

"I like y'all nerve! What makes y'all think y'all can butt the line?"

"Must be those monkey suits, girl. Maybe they the waiters."

The crowd laughed. The doorman was not amused.

"We not letting anybody in for another half hour. Line starts in the rear."

Hopson tried to look around the six-four, 240-pound door-man. "I need to get in there now. It's important. I have to see Imani."

"Everybody in line is waiting to see Imani."

Hopson tried to push past. "It's important."

The doorman grabbed him by the arm and jerked him back. "Man, I ain't no punk you can just walk around. Get to the rear or get hurt."

Sherman tried. "Listen, player. We've got business with Imani. She's expecting us."

"What's your name?"

"I'm Rick Sherman. And he's Orenthal Hopson."

The doorman shook his head. "Ain't on the VIP list."

Sherman reasoned. "Can't you just tell Imani that we're out here?"

"Nope," Tonya and her friend chimed up. These were the lit-tle girls who idolized Imani. "He won't tell her we're here, and we hang out with her at the bus station. We're like her little sisters."

The doorman grunted at her. "Told y'all shorties y'all are *too young* to be in dah club. Go home. And like I *already told them,* man, I'm not bothering Imani before showtime *for nobody.* So it's the end of the line, brah."

"Now, look . . ." Hopson went to push forward again.

Sherman stopped him. "He's right. We'll just have to wait." Sherman reluctantly led Hopson away. "C'mon."

They got back in the car. Hopson told Sherman, "I didn't come all this way to give up."

"Who said anything about giving up? If you can't go *through* the mountain, go *around* it."

Sherman drove them to the end of the block. He turned the corner and made a quick half turn into an alley, stopped short, and parked.

"Now what?" Hopson questioned, the smell of stale urban

life hanging heavy in the air. "Do you know where you're going?"

"Walk," Sherman answered. "And watch where you step."

Sherman led the way until they reached the back of Club Maceo. Hopson reached for the back door. Sherman grabbed his hand. "Locked." Then he motioned with his head. "Through there."

Hopson watched. Sherman turned sideways and sidestepped down a narrow gangway. He sighed and followed. Suddenly there was another door. Sherman put his ear against it. He squeezed the knob and threw his hip just below the keyhole and it opened. "We're in, man."

They walked through the rear storage area where stacks of cognac, gin, and vodka were stored. It opened up into a hallway. The music was pumping. There were people getting the tables ready. A tech was fiddling with the soundboard.

Imani was standing on the newly built stage, giving mike checks. She had on a small black fedora, slanted left. Beneath that was a metallic silver scarf wrapped around her head, tied into a thick bun at the back. She had on big silver hoop earrings, a Raiders black and silver jersey, tight silver pants, and black pumps.

Hopson whispered to Sherman, *"That is so not her anymore."*

"Then go get her."

Hopson walked towards Imani, his eyes fixated on her oasis of talent and beauty. One of the security guards at the front door happened to turn and see him. "Hey. You're not supposed to be in here."

Imani looked up and saw him. "Hops!" She told security, "It's okay."

"This guy too?" he pointed at Sherman.

Imani looked at him and half smiled. "Yeah. He's all right too."

Hopson mounted the stage. "Imani, you don't know how much I've wanted to see you, to talk to you."

"I know why too."

"Huh?"

"Yeah," Imani said, her voice cracking, "you're leaving. You wanna break it off, so you're leaving."

"I'm leaving not because I don't love you."

Imani dropped her head. "Just say good-bye and don't make it worse by making up things to try and help me feel better."

Hopson raised her chin with his fingertips. "I'm not making anything up. I love you. Can we talk later? Right now I need you to come with me to the ball—"

"Is that all you want from me? To perform your damn music?"

"No." He took her in his arms. "No. Listen to me. Imani, I'm not thinking about me. I'm thinking about you. I feel like you need time to yourself. You're changing so much. I don't want you to feel like it's all for me. I want you to want something for yourself, and hopefully, that wanting will eventually include me. But I want to give you space to see. And I couldn't do that and still be around you. I couldn't stand to be near and have to stay away. That's why I quit my job at Arlington."

"Really? Is that really it?"

"Yes, to give you space. To let you grow and decide what you want and need."

"I don't know, Hops. Maybe that's just an excuse. You're the one who wants space. You need space to figure out if you love me or not."

"That's not it, Imani. I'm sure of that."

"Then what's with the space? I don't need it, Hops. I need you to show me how you feel. To be strong around me and let me be strong around you. That's all, Hops. Everything else will work out."

"Are you sure?" Hopson kissed her.

She kissed him. "Yes."

One of Taz's boys was heading to the bar to sneak a drink. He caught the action, stopped, and then began to slip away.

"All you have to do now is come to the ball with me. You've got to perform tonight, Imani."

"After all we just said. Is that all you care about, music and that damn ball?"

"Don't signify, listen. I don't want you to go to the ball for me. I want you to go for you. One of the best music producers in the world is going to be there. Lionel Whitmore."

"Lionel Whitmore?"

"The one and only. Imani, I want him to hear you perform. I want him to know the talent that I know, that I've grown to love. It's for you, girl. For you."

Imani stared into Hopson's eyes.

Sherman walked up, stopping at the foot of the stage. "Imani, I've been standing back there not saying a word. But I gotta jump in now. Don't trip over some B.S. This is your time. Get your gown and c'mon."

Hopson hugged her again and whispered in her ear, "Please."

Tears welled up in her eyes.

Suddenly the house lights went on. Hopson shielded his eyes with one of his hands then struggled to look towards the back of the hall. He couldn't make out the people walking towards them, but he knew in his heart that this would be a showdown.

Chapter Twenty-six

Imani's father, Taz, Claude, and Mr. Watson came marching towards them.

"What the hell is up?" Taz growled. "Get off that stage, man."

Imani and Hopson held each other tighter.

Mr. Watson took measure of the couple and Professor Sherman, who was standing at the foot of the stage.

Claude pegged Hopson for a punk. "I'll throw his ass out first, no thang."

Professor Hopson pushed Imani away, squared his shoulders. *He was down.*

But Sherman had his boy's back. "You'll have to go through me first." He glared at Claude and Mr. Watson. "We ain't no punks. Bring it."

Claude opened his jacket and showed off two pistols. "Which one you wanna get shot with?"

"Ice that." Mr. Watson put the brakes on Claude. He looked around the room at the help. "Everybody out of here, now. To the back."

The workers cleared the room. Mr. Watson slowly pulled out a cigar, lit it, and sat down. "What's the trouble?"

"No trouble." Hopson shrugged. "Imani's coming with me. She's not performing here tonight."

"Imani?" her father, Maceo, questioned. He was so stunned he plopped down in the nearest chair. "That true, baby?"

Taz shouted, "She ain't going nowhere!"

Mr. Watson decided to roll down the easy route. "Imani, we had a deal. I've got a lot of money tied up in this. You've got people waiting outside. They paid their money."

"I know that," Imani said fiercely.

"And what about your father? You wanna lose this club for him?"

Imani glanced lovingly at her father. "I'd never do anything to hurt my daddy."

"Baby, c'mere." Maceo held out his arms. Imani climbed down off the stage and went to him. He took her hands as he sat. Imani stood in front of him. "Remember the other night, we were talking about loyalty? And I started to say something but didn't?"

She nodded.

"What I was gonna say then, I need to say now. Imani, don't ever let loyalty to someone else destroy your dreams. Never let anyone or anything stand in the way of your dreams, baby. A person without dreams can't do nothing for themselves and won't have anything to give somebody else."

"What are you trying to say, Daddy?"

"I'm saying that you don't owe me anything but the love a daughter has for her father. You didn't ask to come here. Your mama and I brought you here. We owed you a proper upbringing. You owed us respect if we pulled it off."

Taz spoke bitterly. "You telling her to go, Maceo? That's wrong, man. Imani, why don't you stop letting this weak-ass professor pull your string? You belong down here on the low end on that stage rapping your heart out. You belong with me, Imani."

"No I don't," Imani said defiantly. "I don't, Taz."

"What?! Aww, girl. I can't believe you're turning on a brother like this." He slapped his chest. "Me. Taz."

"I'm not turning on anybody." She stepped forward. "I'm not going to the ball for Hops. I'm not trying to mess you over, Taz, or disrespect you, Daddy, or let you down, Mr. Watson. I'm trying to do what's right for me. To sing my song. To be my own woman here in my own time, making my own decisions. That's what I have to do. It took a while, a lot of running into brick walls, but that's what I realized. That's what I know."

"That's bull and you know it, Imani."

"Taz, aren't you the one who says you do what you have to do? If you really believe that, then it should be good for me just like it is for you."

"I ain't trying to hear that. This is about us, girl, you and me."

"Naw, baby . . . this is about what *you* need and want. Let me tell you about what you have. All the other performers you're producing are dying to be on that stage tonight throwing down your tracks. I'm not one of them, Taz. Go with them."

"So it's like that? You leaving me hanging?"

"I want to find what's right for me. Is that so wrong?"

"Imani, I'm not gonna stand here and beg your ass. I'm not."

"Baby, please don't."

Taz looked at Imani. "All right. All right fine, then. G'on and do what you gotta do, then."

She stepped towards him and raised her hand to his cheek. Taz turned his back and dropped his head. "G'on."

Imani felt a tinge of sadness in her gut. "No matter what, Taz, we still family. Know that, hear? Know that?"

Taz still wouldn't look at her. Imani glanced at her father whose eyes were warm and supportive. "That's fine with me, baby," Maceo said. "G'on and do your thang."

Hopson jumped down from the stage and took Imani by the hand to lead her away.

Claude blocked their path and pulled out his pistols. "Well it ain't all right with us."

Sherman stepped over and turned his body towards the pistols and faced Mr. Watson. "I take it this is about what's owed?"

Mr. Watson leaned back and pulled out a cigar, lit it.

"This is about what one person owes another, right? You want Imani to pay the debt for her father."

Mr. Watson blew a ring of smoke over Sherman's head.

"What about the debt a father owes to a son?"

Mr. Watson didn't venture a syllable.

"Goddamn it, answer me!" Sherman yelled at him.

Claude aimed the pistols sideways. "Man, you crazy? Who the hell you think you talkin' to like that up in here?"

"My father," Sherman answered. He didn't take his eyes off Mr. Watson. He spoke over his shoulder. "Hey Hopson, did you wonder how I knew this area so well? How I knew about that trick side door? I used to live down here when I was little, before my mother took me away."

"Lord have mercy," Maceo said, squinting. "I remember you now. You're Watson's boy, Rick. You used to be a little old something running down around here. This was way before Imani was born. I wondered what happened to you."

"My mother took me away. When I got to be a teenager I snuck back down here a couple of times to see my father. The last time I was about, oh, sixteen years old. I'd won a music contest and wanted to show him the medal they gave me. He turned me away like it was nothing. I got so mad I threw the medal at him. He didn't give a good goddamn."

Mr. Watson leaned back in his chair. "You thought I didn't care? Your mother took you away because she didn't want you to turn out like me. What could I do, son?"

"Fight for me. Fight to be with me."

"I couldn't get a lawyer and fight for custody, expose my

business, have people digging around. I'd ah wound up in jail and then what good would that do?"

"*Excuses, excuses. You just didn't give a damn.*"

"Son, your mother wouldn't let me near you. She'd call and brag on you though. So I knew about all the fine things you were doing. She even sent me a photo of you getting your PhD. Biggie saw it at my house. Told me he saw you, recognized you that night when he and Taz went after the professor here in the parking lot."

"That's why he backed off so quick," Taz mumbled.

"Yeah." Mr. Watson nodded, putting out his cigar. "That's why. I stayed away, son, but I never, never stopped caring."

Sherman's chest was heaving up and down as he listened. "I wish I could believe that."

Mr. Watson stood up, reached into his pocket, and walked over to Sherman. He pulled on the chain that looped from his waist to his pocket. At the end of the chain was the round gold piece he had a habit of playing with. He held it up to Sherman. "It's a little worn but tell me, what does that say?"

Sherman could barely read the writing. When he did his voice cracked. " 'First place. State Music Semifinals.' "

"I never stopped caring."

The two men continued to look into each other's eyes.

Hopson spoke softly but firm. "We've got to go." He looked from Claude to Mr. Watson. "We've got to go *now* if we're going to make it in time for the performance."

Sherman challenged his father. "What about it? It's on you."

"*No it's not,*" Imani dared. "It's on me. We're going."

Mr. Watson laughed. "You go, baby girl." Then he took his hand and lowered Claude's weapons. "Go on."

Claude jerked around. "Huh? C'mon, Mr. Watson. You can't just let them go. You slipping, man!"

Mr. Watson smiled, then let that smile turn into a sneer.

"You're right, Claude. I *was* slipping. Past tense. Like, not paying attention to your collection money. Your kitty has been light but somehow your pockets have been getting fatter and fatter."

"What's up?" Claude faked innocence. "I ain't feeling you."

"You will be. I know you've been stealing!" Mr. Watson shouted. "Boys!"

Claude's eyes orbed like mad in his head, getting large and darting from left to right.

Three of Mr. Watson's other enforcers stepped from behind the doorway, guns already drawn.

"And what about Biggie, Claude? What about him?"

Claude shrugged. "He all right, just in the hospital."

"And you put him there."

"Naw, Mr. Watson."

Mr. Watson backhanded Claude across the face then snatched the pistols out of his slumping hands. He berated him. "You shot Biggie because he started asking a lot of questions, you knew he'd come to me if he found out anything. A druggie in the alley saw you running away after the shooting. Turned you in for the reward money I offered."

"Mr. Watson, you gonna believe some crackhead instead of me? This is Claude, man. I'm your niggah."

"I know you. And I've been snooping around myself, long before Biggie. You're a thief. So yeah, Claude, I know you. You did it. Now ya gotta pay."

Sweat began cascading down Claude's forehead and neck. "C'mon, man . . . all these years . . . they gotta mean something, please . . ."

"Handle him, boys." Mr. Watson sighed. "I must be slipping 'cause I can't green-light you, can't have 'em kill you like I should. Naw, you're banished, Claude. You're out of the game in this city, player. But when they get through with you, I'll be damned if you steal from somebody else. *Ever.*"

They hustled Claude out.

Mr. Watson seemed in a trance. He finally focused on Hopson and Imani.

"We're going," Imani said defiantly.

Mr. Watson smiled. "I don't think I could stop you even if I wanted to. I gotta feeling that *can't nobody* stop you."

Imani's eyes sparkled. She and Hopson turned to leave. Sherman didn't move. He reached into his pocket and tossed Hopson his car keys. "Y'all go without me. I have some catching up to do here."

Chapter Twenty-seven

How do you make up for lost time, cover new ground? Does it have to be figured out like an equation or a riddle? Or is a willing and able spirit enough?

Imani and Hopson had lost time—oh not like Sherman and his father—not so much in terms of years, days, even hours, but in terms of the time that two people discover that they're truly in sync with each other. They'd been so close, so close to being on beat, to being in time, but fear and insecurity proved to be a more powerful magnet. It was a magnet of extreme negative force, pulling them apart, leaving them longing like empty, out-stretched arms. Could they finally fill those arms for each other?

Imani dressed quickly while Hopson waited outside in the car. As hurried as they were, Imani had the confidence and the care to take the space she needed to stop and examine herself in the full-length mirror. She stepped back, startled, and oh so very pleased. Imani saw a glorious self. She saw inner beauty and outer beauty together. Imani finally had the hook-up.

Her desire to succeed started to simmer within her soul. Imani felt it, loved the feel of it, and hoped the best hope that it would overtake her. At last, Imani was ready.

She stepped into the night, wearing a scarf over her head and a cape around her shoulders. The cape was older, not very pretty, yet it was comforting as a quilt, a piece of her mother's clothing that had survived the fire. Imani didn't want anyone to fully glimpse the new her until she stepped up to perform.

Hopson drove the car like he was in an action scene from the movie *The Fast and the Furious*. The swift watch of opportunity was ticking away. Could they make it in time?

Back at the ball, Chairman Perkins held court with two of Arlington's chief benefactors, along with Lionel Whitmore.

"Almost time for the performance." Chairman Perkins checked his watch. "How's your wine, Lionel?"

Lionel Whitmore took a big gulp, grinned, and said, "Not as good as my grandfather used to make for first communion, but it's the next best thing." Then he turned and laughed for the camera.

A benefactor cooed, "We're so glad you're here, Mr. Whitmore. What a surprise."

"Call me Lionel. Please. I've always missed this ball. You get so busy sometimes that you forget about making time for the things that are important and good. I wish I could stay for the entire evening but I've got a plane to catch."

"We appreciate any time that you can give us, Lionel." Chairman Perkins postured. "The music department appreciates your support. I think you'll see that this year's jazz band is one of our greatest."

"That'll be soon, I hope."

"Right now, in fact. I'll run back and get things started."

Behind the curtained stage, Hopson was talking with the jazz band. Most of them were in his composition class. He was handing them arrangements for the songs that he and Imani had spent weeks preparing. She was in a dressing room touching up her makeup and getting focused.

Chairman Perkins arrived backstage and went off. "Professor Hopson! What in the hell do you think you're doing?"

"Chairman Perkins. Oh, good. Listen, there's going to be a change."

"*What kind of a change?* Did you quit or did you not, Professor?"

"It's not about that. Listen, Imani's here. She's going to perform."

"The hell she is." The veins in Chairman Perkins's neck were throbbing. "Lionel Whitmore is out there with a *film crew.*"

"I know. That's why Imani *has* to perform."

"Forget it. No way, Professor."

Hopson grabbed him. "Don't take it out on her because you're mad at me. Let Imani perform, please."

"Do you think everything is about you? Well it isn't. You've been a selfish ass, sir. I'm thinking about Arlington. This is a wonderful opportunity for this university. If Imani's performance goes to hell, they'll cut the school out of the film altogether. What will our benefactors say then? The trustees? Arlington can't risk that!"

"Where's your faith, Chairman?"

"Where's yours, Professor? *You're* the one who *quit!* You seem to be one of the new talented tenth that thinks the grass is greener on the *white side* of the picket fence. Go to the Ivy League or the Big Ten. I don't give a damn. Arlington was here before you, it'll be here after you."

"But Chairman . . ."

"Security! Security!"

The security guard, whom Hopson and Sherman had given such a hard time about Imani, stepped forward. Chairman Perkins gave the order. "This man no longer works here. He's to be escorted off the property. Let all the guards know he's not to be let back into the ball under any circumstances."

"My pleasure!" The guard grabbed Hopson and began dragging him away.

"Give Imani a chance! She's earned it!"

Chairman Perkins ignored Hopson's pleas. The old guy had his surly side up and sharpened to a point. He walked around and began snatching Hopson's arrangements off the music stands.

Ahmad, one of the campus leaders, and the most popular person in the band, tried to reason with Chairman Perkins. "But Chairman, wait. Imani has been working hard. We've all seen her. Can't we just let her sing one song?"

"No, Ahmad."

"But she really is good, Chairman, and we all think she deserves it."

"Ahmad, you'll do as you're told. Find your horn. You *were* going to conduct tonight but it looks to me like I better take over. I don't want any funny stuff."

"But Chairman—"

He played Ahmad off and barked out orders: "Places. Everyone to your places and get ready."

Ahmad glanced from one band member to the next. Just as they all fell silent, Imani walked up. All eyes settled on her. It took Chairman Perkins more than a moment to compose himself for what he had to do. Only the voice of the trustee who had begun the introduction could press him forward.

"I'm sorry, Imani. You won't be performing here tonight."

Imani's gaze never wavered. "I have a song that I want to perform. It's about some things that I've learned here . . . being secure in who you are . . . having pride in where you come from . . . Isn't that the true tradition of Arlington?"

"Yes . . . but . . . I . . . can't." Chairman Perkins shook his head no. "I just can't."

"You can take this opportunity away from me now, Chairman. That's in your power. But you can't block my blessing. It's going to come. And I'm going to be right here to get it."

"I'm sorry, Imani. It's not just my decision; it's my duty. You may stay and listen to the band if you'd like."

Outside, the security guard grinned as he shoved Hopson away from the rear door. He radioed the chairman's message over the two-way to the other guards. "Well that's that, Professor Hot Shit." He drew his nightstick for emphasis. *"How ya like me now?"*

Hopson cowered and turned as if he were going to walk away, but instead he spun around and punched the security guard right in the mouth. He fell flat on his back. Hopson snapped his fingers in front of the man's face. He was out cold. Hopson asked him, "How you like *me* now?"

Hopson reached for the door to get back inside. It was locked. "Oh God," he moaned.

Inside, the trustee was finishing up his introduction.

"Ladies and gentlemen . . . tonight we have a special treat. The Arlington Jazz Band will perform for your listening pleasure a medley of jazz classics from the early era up to and including recent Grammy winners in the classic jazz category. But first a little history of how this musical group came to be . . ."

Outside, Hopson was scrutinizing the building, trying to take it apart, brick by brick. He knew there were guards at all the doors and none of them would let him back inside. *I've got to get in, but how?* he asked himself. Hopson looked around the base of the building. All the windows had metal security screens on them. *Can't get in there.*

Then Hopson looked up, *way up.* There was an open window. It was near where the lighting engineer sat. It was open to let in some air to cool the equipment. Hopson looked at the flat walls and ran around the side of the building. There was a drainpipe, thick and round, that led up to the window. He whipped off his jacket, spit in his hands, and started to shimmy up.

Inside, the trustee's introduction came to a crescendo. "And now I present to you the Arlington Jazz Band!"

The curtains were drawn back. Chairman Perkins was center stage with the band seated behind him. The crowd of polished well-to-do African-Americans in their tuxes and ball gowns cheered the school's cream of the crop. Chairman Perkins beamed.

"On behalf of the Arlington faculty, on behalf of the jazz band we thank you. Tonight's performance is dedicated to one of the school's most illustrious graduates, Mr. Lionel Whitmore."

The crowd erupted in cheers. A floodlight was *supposed to* engulf him in a soft, yellow light. It didn't. Chairman Perkins quickly tried to cover up the mistake. "Now, to begin our performance tonight. We will start with the school anthem, 'The Song of Arlington.' "

Chairman Perkins turned and raised his conductor's wand. He began to wave his arms but there was no sound. Ahmad and the other students sat as still as stones and didn't raise their instruments.

" 'The Song of Arlington!' " Chairman Perkins blustered. He waved his arms frantically.

Ahmad cut his eyes at Imani in the wings. She smiled and began to sing from off stage, no music, just her powerful voice.

She sang the first words of the song, "Oh Arlington . . ."

Every head in the house was craning trying to see who owned such a slamming voice. The crowd was buzzing. The degreed and the jeweled were mesmerized by the stunning sound that seemed to have an ancestral force behind it: a force as powerful as a set of oars pushing a huge ship of talent forward on a wave of courage. It was Imani. Yeah, it was her.

Up in the rafters, Hopson smiled. The lighting engineer was in the corner counting the money he'd just been paid off with. Hopson flicked the switch for the spotlight and swung it towards the rear of the stage.

Imani saw the light. For her it was a sign that her unique blessing was finally here, being sent down from what seemed like the heavens. In her mind's eye, she saw herself years past, sitting on the fence, watching from the outside looking in. Kept out.

Barred from entering. Not included. But now things were different for Imani. And if she blew the roof off tonight, things could be different for other girls like her too; downtown girls who had the heart and the courage to find themselves, then show that gem to the world.

Imani stepped forward into the light. It was her light all along, meant for her to glow in, to bask in, to share with others. It was straight up her light. Couldn't nobody cut it off and couldn't no amount of player hating dim it. What is for you is for you.

Imani had on a gown that was traditional yet hip. The dress held her breasts and hips like a passionate lover but was respectfully pretty to the eye. The color was a glowing swirl of cream and brown that flowed right into the next degree of sho' nuff dark and lovely that was her copper skin color.

Imani's hair was texturized and twisted in tiny afrocentric rows in the front. The back was swept up in a French roll with cowry shells quilted within the strands. Imani wasn't showing Taz's vision of stage style. She wasn't showing Hopson's vision either. She wasn't rap. She wasn't jazz. She was neo-soul. Imani was herself.

Imani had completed a musical migration. A lost bird, Imani had flown from nest to nest singing others' songs until finally landing on a branch of her own.

Now her voice was a combination of things—its timbre not the least among them—which included volume and emotion. Imani found notes inside of her that had been planted in the womb, growing all this time, waiting to be birthed. She sang and no one said a mumbling word. Not a sound. Not the workers in the kitchen. Not the students in the band. Not even Hopson who was making his way downstage.

He was walking in a stagger, mesmerized by Imani's beauty and talent. Walking forward to a person who had so much love and energy, who he wanted to share all he had with. Stunned at that moment, Hopson had known all along that he loved Imani—just not how much. It happens to most of us if we find true love; some incident, look, word, thought, or situation strikes the heart like a gong and awakens our insides to that special something that's now in our presence.

By the time Hopson reached backstage, Imani had finished and the entire room erupted in raging applause. Even Chairman Perkins was clapping like it was Sunday and he had the Holy Ghost.

Hopson walked onto the stage with tears in his eyes. Chairman Perkins looked at him, nodded, and gave way. Hopson took the mike.

"Ladies and gentlemen, that voice you just heard belongs to Imani Holland, a local performer soon to take the world by storm with her enormous talent and her breathtaking beauty. I've had the extreme pleasure, the incredible luck, to work with Imani over the past couple of months. I have learned from her and I admire her. She is one fine lady."

Hopson gave way.

Imani pointed to the music rack and Hopson pulled out the music sheets. He looked surprised then began handing them out to the band members. Imani spoke to the crowd.

"I am so honored to be here this evening. I've dreamed of this since I was a little girl . . ."

And as she said those words, Imani closed her eyes and saw herself as a child again, sitting on the fence, looking in the window smiling . . . Imani got choked up but managed to open her eyes and carry on now, for she had a dream, a purpose . . .

"I'm sure you don't realize it, but I've been here before. I wasn't working out back in the kitchen. Or in the audience wearing a fine gown. I wasn't onstage either. I was just outside the window, on the fence, watching, listening, and dreaming of performing one day in front of a crowd like this . . . a crowd of beautiful, smart, accomplished people . . . God and, I'd like to think, my mother in heaven have granted me this wish. This song is about the love I've felt here at Arlington and the pride I've seen behind these walls . . . This one is for you all."

And she *sang*.

Imani began singing her mother's song. She had worked long and hard over the words, over the arrangement. And it was paying off big-time. Imani's voice leapt from the depths of her soul, cascading around the room. Her range and her poise mesmerized everyone at the ball—especially all of the trained music men. Her voice appeared as if from some era past: steady and strong, hallowed and haunting. Each note struck the ceiling and bounced down to the floor then back up again, hanging in midair, hovering with the greatest of power.

Imani sang out of proof, out of anger and hurt and disappointment. And instead of tears, she shed notes that hadn't been hit by a set of lungs in years.

When Imani finished, the crowd showered her with gratitude that leapt from the heat of their hands pounding together and from their throats screaming praise.

Lionel Whitmore was at the edge of the stage. The noise was so loud she could barely hear him. He shouted so she could hear and he exalted so she could truly believe. "Imani, you are a star. I have a plane to catch but tomorrow morning I want you to call my private line. We've got to talk about your future. You are a star!"

Imani spun around with joy. Hopson kissed her passionately. Whitmore laughed and threw his hand up and Hopson slapped him five. "You're the man!" Then he vanished into the crowd.

Chairman Perkins stepped up behind Hopson and cleared his throat. "Uhhh-humphf! Just because Lionel Whitmore thinks *you're the man,* doesn't mean that I'll take you back on staff here. I assume that is what you want?"

Imani cuddled closer to Hopson and nodded yes.

"Sir, I'll do my best to make Arlington proud . . ."

"You already have, son. Keep it up. Oh. And about our bet . . ."

"That's right." Hopson grinned. "I win, Chairman. I was right."

"No, you were wrong. I'm going to enter Professor Sherman's paper in the grant contest."

"But Imani's performance is the proof."

"It wasn't the music that changed her, Professor. It was love. Love of self. Sorry, but you lose. And I know you hate to lose."

Imani let her head fall gently on Hopson's shoulder. He smiled. "Well . . . if this is losing, I'll take a loss every time."

Chairman Perkins bowed slightly from the waist. "Ms. Imani, a waltz with you later, please?"

"Absolutely."

There was a break between the concert and the beginning of the traditional waltz. The crowd was buzzing and mingling, talking about what they'd just heard.

"Imani, I'll take my dance now."

"Now? But there's no music."

Hopson remembered what his grandfather told his grandmother years ago in the basement of their home. He repeated it now to Imani, "Baby . . . you're my song."

And they danced.

Epilogue

"*C*ome on! We're gonna miss Imani" Tonya shouted to her friend, running as fast as she could. The two downtown girls were flying through the night.

They headed to the university because they had heard that Imani wasn't rapping at Club Maceo tonight ... Imani was going to the university ball to perform. That university right up the road with its wrought-iron gates and its proud students, every book they carried as thick as a Webster's dictionary.

Tonya and her friend climbed the fence and peered into the window. Slowly a smile crept across their faces. It was as if the universe was saying, "All things are possible ..."

The downtown girls smiled and watched, almost holding their breath, as if on the other side of the vision before them was a feasible future for any talented colored girl who tried.

They both watched intently and hoped deep down within themselves. "Someday ... yeah ... someday."

Children are blessed because they can dream with their eyes wide open.

Yolanda Joe is the author of four acclaimed novels, including *The Hatwearer's Lesson* and the *Essence* bestsellers *This Just In, Bebe's By Golly Wow,* and *He Say, She Say.* A graduate of the Columbia School of Journalism and a former news producer, she lives in Chicago.